MISSING IN COTTONWOOD SPRINGS

A Cottonwood Springs Cozy Mystery - Book 4

BY

DIANNE HARMAN

Published by: Dianne Harman
www.dianneharman.com

Interior, cover design and website by
Vivek Rajan

ISBN: 9781794603813

CONTENTS

ACKNOWLEDGMENTS

To my family, for their everlasting encouragement and faith in me, thank you!

To my readers, who buy and borrow my books, thank you!

To all the people who contributed their expertise in making this book possible, thank you!

And to my in-house editor and best friend, Tom, thank you!

Win FREE Paperbacks every week!

Go to www.dianneharman.com/freepaperback.html and get your FREE copies of Dianne's books and favorite recipes immediately by signing up for her newsletter.

Once you've signed up for her newsletter you're eligible to win three paperbacks. One lucky winner is picked every week. Hurry before the offer ends!

PROLOGUE

Brigid checked her watch as she hurried to her car. She was running late this morning, and that wasn't like her. She always strived to be on time. Being late for an appointment was one of her pet peeves. That's why normally she would have left twenty minutes earlier, but instead, here she was, rushing out the door well after when she should have left.

There were a number of things that contributed to why she was running late, all of which seemed to have been conspiring against her that day. She'd gotten up later than usual, and because it was a warm day, Jett, her 125-pound Newfoundland dog, hadn't wanted to come inside. Instead, he'd opted for playing in a mud puddle. That was probably for the best, though, because she wouldn't have had time to bathe the big Newfoundland if he had come inside.

"I hope Olivia's not too impatient, because it looks like I'm a little late for my appointment with her" Brigid said aloud to herself as she pulled out of her driveway. For the last few weeks she'd been making plans for her wedding, which just added to her stress level.

Although she was getting close to making some decisions, there were a number still left to be made. More than once, she'd thought about just forgetting about having a wedding and instead, heading to the courthouse for a quick ceremony performed by a clerk. Whenever she verbalized that thought, Holly, her semi-adopted daughter, was quick to remind her that deep down Brigid really didn't want to do that.

And Holly was right. Brigid had been looking forward to planning her dream wedding. With her first husband, her mother-in-law hadn't allowed her to do anything she'd wanted to do like having an outdoor wedding and sunflowers for the floral arrangements. No, almost everything she'd wanted had been quickly vetoed.

Thinking back, Brigid thought she should have paid more attention, because the signs had all been there, practically in neon with bright flashing lights. But she'd been young then, and she'd allowed her mother-in-law to run the show, not wanting to rock the boat. This time, though, she was going to do what she wanted. Well, and what Linc, her husband-to-be wanted too, although he seemed very content to keep repeating, "Whatever you want, Brigid."

Just the thought of his total trust in her had Brigid smiling as she turned onto the town square. She pulled up in front of the flower shop, Ford's Flowers. Owned by Olivia and Mike Ford, it wasn't the only flower shop in Cottonwood Springs, but it was the most popular. From what Fiona said, Olivia's bouquet arrangements were unlike any others. Brigid had never seen any of Olivia's work, but she trusted her sister. If Fiona said she was good, Brigid believed it. Holly had claimed she was impressed by the florist's work as well. If the two most important females in Brigid's life spoke highly of the woman, then that was good enough for Brigid.

She parked her car, climbed out, and walked across the sidewalk towards the front door. "*That's odd*," she thought as she approached the door. All of the lights were still off, even though the sign on the door said they opened at 8:00 am. She looked at her watch to check the time. It read 8:30. She turned to see if anyone was heading in her direction as she scanned the nearby streets, but it appeared that everyone was simply moving along to wherever they were going. Nobody looked as if they were hurrying to meet her. Resigning herself to wait and grateful she wasn't the only one having a busy morning, Brigid contemplated her next step.

She sat down on a cute little wood and cast-iron bench in front of the flower shop window to wait for Olivia. She admired the black metal scrollwork and intricate design, tracing her finger along the pattern. "She's probably just running late, too," Brigid said aloud to herself. She pulled out her phone and began to pass the time. It wasn't often she had a little free time to do absolutely nothing, so she figured she might as well make the most of it.

After swapping fruit in her favorite Match 3 game for a while, a truck pulled up and parked beside her car. Assuming it was Olivia, Brigid tucked her phone back in her purse and stood up. Rather than a young woman climbing out of the silver truck, a disheveled young man got out. His blonde hair looked as though he hadn't combed it that morning, and his clothes looked as though they'd been crumpled on the floor before he pulled them on. He rushed to the door, seemingly unaware that Brigid was standing almost next to it.

"Excuse me," Brigid said as he unlocked the door. He turned, apparently noticing her for the first time.

"I'm sorry," he said apologetically. "Are you the woman Olivia was supposed to meet this morning?"

"Yes," Brigid said. "I'm terribly sorry. I was running a little late. Is she here?"

"No, I'm afraid not," he said. "I'm Mike Ford, her husband. Something's happened to her. Olivia's missing." He pushed open the door to the shop and waved Brigid inside. "Wait right here, and I'll turn on the lights."

Brigid nodded and watched as the man disappeared into the inky blackness of the dark store. His wife was missing? What did he mean by that? Surely she'd just stopped somewhere and forgotten they had an appointment. Cottonwood Springs wasn't exactly a big city where people went missing regularly. There were only so many places a person could go in the small town.

The lights kicked on one by one until the store was fully

illuminated, the fluorescent tubes buzzed overhead as they warmed up. Now that she could see, Brigid looked around, taking in everything the little shop had to offer. There were cherubs and potted plants near the front window. Stuffed animals and other potted flowers lined the walls. Figurines, candies, and almost everything else you could think of to send with flowers filled the space. With so many options and ideas, it was no wonder why the place was so popular. It smelled like springtime with all the flowers. Brigid inhaled deeply, loving the scent of the flower shop which made her feel calm and refreshed.

Mike reappeared from the back, apologizing. "I'm sorry, I really don't know what to say at this point." He brushed his hand over his face. "I planned to just come in and put up a sign. I completely forgot she was supposed to meet with you until I noticed you standing near the door. What was your name again?"

"Brigid Barnes."

"Brigid, that name seems familiar. Aren't you the woman who's helped catch a couple of murderers? The sheriff, Corey Davis, is a friend of mine and he's mentioned you to me a couple of times," he said as he moved around the store. Each time he stopped moving, he adjusted something, like sliding a figurine over a few inches or restacking a display of cards. He seemed filled with anxious energy.

Brigid smiled and said, "One and the same." She was starting to get used to people knowing who she was from the times she'd helped the sheriff's department. For the most part, it had been a blessing in disguise. More people trusted her because of it, but it was a double-edged sword. They also seemed to think she was some sort of miracle worker.

"Have you ever helped find a missing person?" he asked eagerly, his nervous energy pausing for the moment.

Brigid replied hesitantly, "Well, no. I haven't. But the sheriff…," she began but Mike cut her off.

"Would you be willing to help? I'm really worried something bad has happened to Olivia. I'm afraid the longer we wait, the less likely we are to find her," he said. His bright blue eyes fixed intently on Brigid, and she couldn't help but fidget in response.

"Perhaps," Brigid said cautiously. She didn't know much about looking for a missing person, but she didn't imagine it would be any harder than looking for a killer. "I understand your concern. What can you tell me?"

Mike sighed. He seemed to visibly shrink as he calmed himself. "Olivia left the house early this morning. She was going to stop by the store before coming here. She told me she needed to pick up a few things for the day. Normally I come in with her, but today we were taking separate vehicles, because I built a new display case, and it wouldn't fit in her car. I was bringing it in my truck.

"She was going to come here first, so she could clear some space in the shop for it. When I got here this morning and she wasn't here, I went straight to the grocery store. She'd been at the store, because one of the cashiers remembered her leaving. The thing is, her car's still in the parking lot. Her shopping bags were in the front seat of it, but there was no sign of her anywhere. Like I said, Sheriff Davis is a good friend of mine, and he said he'd take a look at the security footage of the grocery store and call me when he knew something."

Brigid's mind began to work. *So she went to the store and disappeared from the parking lot,* she thought. *If her bags were in the front seat of her car, she obviously made it back to her car, but what happened after that? It didn't sound like this was one of those missing persons cases where the person didn't want to be found. Otherwise, why would she leave her car behind?* Brigid wasn't sure what was going on, but she knew she couldn't just sit back and do nothing when she'd been asked to help.

"I'll see what I can do," she finally said.

"Thanks, I really appreciate it. I'm sure you're busy, but everyone seems to think that if a case is going to be solved, it needs to be done quickly. At this point, that's what I need, someone who can help me.

I need my wife back home and safe in my arms," Mike said, his eyes beginning to tear up.

While she was no missing persons detective, Brigid knew she'd been instrumental in helping to solve several cases involving murder investigations. People talked to her. The sheriff said people often opened up to someone who wasn't in law enforcement. If that was so, maybe she could help figure out what happened to Olivia.

CHAPTER ONE

Brigid was sitting in the office she had in her home, trying to get some work done, when Holly walked in. Despite it being almost noon, Holly was still dressed in her pajamas. Her long blonde hair was in a floppy ponytail that looked as though she'd slept with it that way. It was spring break and apparently, she planned to take full advantage of it.

"Remember how I told you I had an aunt in Missouri? My mom's sister?" she asked as she perched one hip on the edge of Brigid's desk.

"Yes," the older woman said. She slid her glasses off her nose and up into her red hair. She leaned back in her chair to listen to Holly. "What about her?"

"She sent me a message online," she said as she scrolled through her phone. "I guess she wants to meet me."

"Really?" Brigid asked, feeling a slight twinge of worry. "Why's that?"

"She said she'd heard about Mom, and also that I was being well taken care of, but she didn't like not knowing who I was or anything about me. I guess Sheriff Davis talked to her after Mom died and filled her in on the situation. She said she understood and respected that, but it's been eating at her that she doesn't know me and asked if I'd like to visit her and her family. I mean, that makes sense, right?"

Brigid could tell by Holly's tone of voice that she really wanted to know what Brigid thought. Her first, knee-jerk reaction was to feel hurt. After all, she'd been taking care of Holly ever since her mother had been murdered in a local church. Why, all of a sudden, did this woman in Missouri want to get to know Holly? Yet on the other hand, how could she blame her? She was family, after all. What if she had a niece that she never got to see because her sister had moved away? Brigid knew she'd do the same thing.

"And how do you feel about it?" Brigid asked. She'd learned that with teenagers it's always wise to see what their opinion is on something before speaking yours. Otherwise, they may take whatever you said the wrong way. She didn't want to hurt Holly's feelings or make it seem as though she wasn't supportive, because she was. Yet she knew it was a very touchy subject, and she wasn't sure how Holly might be feeling about it.

"I wouldn't mind meeting some of my family," Holly said. "I never knew who my dad was, so it was always just me and my mom. I never saw pictures of these people except for the one I got from the trailer where Mom and I lived, and that one was pretty old. It might be nice to see what they're like. You know, meet my cousins and stuff like that."

Brigid could see that Holly was interested, but she had a feeling Holly didn't want to hurt her feelings. She stood up from her desk and pulled the girl into her arms. Brigid had always known this might happen. She just wasn't ready for it to happen so soon.

"Then I think it's a great idea. They are family, after all. Maybe it'll give you a chance to learn more about where you came from." Brigid pulled Holly closer. "Maybe you could visit them while Linc and I go on our honeymoon?"

"That's a great idea, Brigid!" Holly gasped. "It'll be summer vacation, and you won't have to worry about me while you're gone.

Oh, but what about Jett?" she blurted out, referring to Brigid's 125-pound Newfoundland dog.

"Fiona's already offered to take him while we're gone," Brigid said. "So that's all worked out. Go ahead and tell your aunt it's fine. If we can plan far enough ahead, we can get cheaper airline tickets for you." She gave Holly's arm a strong supportive squeeze.

"Okay," Holly said brightly as she bounced out of the office. Brigid heard her squeal with happiness as she hurried back down the hall, retreating to her own room.

Brigid smiled to herself. She did feel protective about Holly, but in reality, her relatives were probably great people. She acknowledged the slight flutter of fear in her heart when she considered that Holly might like it there and not want to come back, but she tried to ignore it. There was no need to worry about something that hadn't even cropped up yet. More than likely, there had been some silly falling out and Holly's mother had distanced herself from her family.

If there were angry feelings, Holly's mother probably hadn't talked about them much, if at all. Top that off with her being an absent parent, and it was no wonder Holly really knew nothing about her extended family. She deserved to be surrounded by as many supportive and loving people as she could get. Considering how great of a kid she was after everything she'd been through, Brigid felt she'd earned that right.

Brigid's talk with Holly had distracted her from work and now her mind was flooded with thoughts of the wedding. She'd almost forgotten how overwhelming it was to plan a wedding. The cake, the venue, flowers, dresses, the whole thing made her head want to explode. It wasn't that she was worried about getting married. No, that was the easy part.

She was absolutely certain that Linc was the perfect guy for her. He was young at heart, smart, and incredibly kind and generous. The fact he was very easy on the eyes didn't hurt either. Yet, for some reason, as she tried to make wedding plans, she became overcome with anxiety. It was much easier to postpone the plans and focus on something else. She knew she couldn't do that forever, but for now, it was how she was dealing with it.

Thinking of wedding plans, she glanced at the clock again and counted how much time she had before Linc came over from his house next door. They were going to look at a potential venue for the ceremony. Neither one of them was too excited about having a church ceremony, since both of them had been married in churches for their first marriages. Obviously, they hadn't turned out well. Instead, they were hoping for something outdoors and a little more intimate. After all, late spring in the Rockies can be spectacularly beautiful, so why not take advantage of it?

There was a nature reserve not too far from Cottonwood Springs that was a popular venue for weddings. Brigid wasn't sure she wanted to get married in the same place so many others had, but she and Linc had decided to look at it. After all, there had to be a reason it was so popular. They'd made an appointment for later that day. The pictures she'd seen of it were beautiful, which was why she decided to give it a shot. Although she normally wasn't one who liked to do what everyone else had done, she thought seeing it in person might make her feel differently.

Brigid let out a long sigh as she thought about all the things she had to do, and then pressed the save button on her computer to save the document she was proofreading and closed down her computer. She had about an hour until Linc would be there. It was time for her to get ready.

She stood up from her desk, stretched her back, and took a deep breath. Things had been very calm lately in Cottonwood Springs, and everyone thought that was a good thing. Brigid wasn't so sure. She was hoping for a little excitement to take her mind off the wedding and Holly's trip. Of course, she didn't want anyone to get murdered, but a little change of pace from the calm would be nice.

As she stepped out of her office, Jett, her massive black Newfoundland, began to whine.

"What's the matter, Jett?" she asked. He turned and rushed to the back door, letting her know that he needed to be let outside.

"I should really think about getting you a doggie door," she said aloud to herself as she let him out.

"Can you imagine the size of it?" Holly asked as she came shuffling into the great room. She had the same shirt on, but she'd managed to put on a pair of jeans. "That thing would practically be big enough for a human door."

"You're right," Brigid said. "It probably wouldn't be very practical with our cold winters, either."

"Agreed," Holly said with a laugh. She took a few steps forward and started fidgeting with the pillows on the couch. Brigid could tell she was about to ask for something or perhaps a favor. "Can I ride my bike over to Wade's house?" Holly finally asked after adjusting the last pillow.

"Is anyone else going to be there?" Brigid trusted Holly to be responsible, but she remembered what it was like to be a teenager. It was better to check and be certain, than assume she'd be given all the details.

"Of course," Holly said as she rolled her eyes. Brigid laughed. She knew Holly didn't mean anything by it. She often rolled her eyes when she thought something was so glaringly obvious she shouldn't have to spell it out.

"That's fine. You don't have to go to the nature reserve to check it out with us."

"You're not going to choose it, so I'd just be wasting my time, anyway," Holly said definitively.

"Oh? Why do you say that?" Brigid asked as she arched an eyebrow.

"I visited it when we were on a field trip back in the fifth grade. It's not you," she said as she sent a text on her phone. She returned to her bedroom, presumably to finish getting ready. Brigid figured it was Wade that she'd been texting.

Brigid thought about what Holly had said. She'd never been to the reserve, even when she'd been in school in Cottonwood Springs all those years ago. As a matter of fact, she didn't recall ever going on a field trip when she was in school. Oh well, she'd try and keep an open mind, no matter what Holly had said.

As she went down the hall to her bedroom to get ready, Brigid began whistling "Here comes the bride." If she was going to be doing wedding things, she might as well get in the mood.

CHAPTER TWO

Brigid had just finished getting ready when she heard Linc knocking on the front door. She unlocked it and started to open it while Jett ran around her, trying to get to Linc. He always seemed to know when it was Linc on the other side of the door.

"Calm down, Jett," she said, laughing. The dog barked excitedly, pressing his face into the crack as Brigid opened the door.

"Hey, big guy," Linc said, ruffling the fur on the giant dog's head. "You being good?" He looked over at Brigid, smiled, gave her a kiss, and said, "Are you about ready?"

"Yes, let me tell Holly we're leaving," she said as she turned around. She hurried down the hall to Holly's room, and knocked on the door.

Holly was sliding on her shoes while she opened the door. "Linc's here. Make sure you put Jett out before you leave and lock the door behind you," Brigid reminded her.

"I know. I will," Holly said smiling. "Have fun checking out a place you aren't going to pick."

Brigid rolled her eyes, but laughed. "Hey, you never know," she said pointing her finger at Holly.

"Yeah, I do. You're not going to pick it." Holly was having a good time teasing Brigid about her inability to find what she wanted.

"We'll see," Brigid said as she walked away. Once she was back in the great room, she hoisted her purse over her shoulder and told Linc, "I'm as ready as I'll ever be."

They left the house and climbed into Linc's truck. The cold winter months were behind them, finally, and warmer weather was starting to make its debut. Early spring flowers were popping out of the ground, and the trees were starting to bud. Brigid couldn't wait until everything was in full bloom.

"What are you thinking about?" Linc asked as they drove through town.

"How ready I am for spring to really get here. Maybe I'll feel a little more enthusiastic about planning our wedding when everything is fresher," she sighed.

"You know, we don't have to do all of this, if you don't want to. I want you to plan the wedding you want, not what you think we should have." Linc reached across the seat and took Brigid's hand in his. A warm, loving feeling spread through her chest as she laced her fingers between his. Just the touch of his hand soothed her frazzled nerves. She hadn't even realized how tense she was until he reached out and touched her.

"I know. That's what I'm trying to do, but nothing seems to feel right. I can't seem to settle on anything." She turned back toward the window and watched the town fade into the countryside. "I want to do something that represents who we are, and how we've managed to get to where we are today. I'm starting to wonder if I even know what that is."

Brigid had begun to think she was being too picky. Could it be she hadn't been able to make any decisions because she was subconsciously afraid of getting married again? She silently shook her head. Maybe she'd been reading too many self-help books lately.

"You do. That's why nothing has felt right. You know exactly what you want, but it just hasn't made itself known yet. Don't stress over it. You'll figure it out and when you do, everything will fall into place." He squeezed her hand reassuringly.

"You think?" she asked.

"I know," he said confidently. Brigid couldn't believe how lucky she was. Sometimes she wished she'd met Linc years ago, but she always tried to push those thoughts away. She knew she'd been a different woman then. Maybe things worked out the way they did because of divine timing. Their time was now, and she was going to soak it all up to the maximum extent possible.

When they pulled into the nature reserve, Brigid tried to imagine showing up there on her wedding day. The office consisted of a short, brown building that resembled a log cabin. Granted, it was much nicer than the average cabin, and its natural beauty blended nicely with the various greenery and floral arrangements. She could envision a bridal party scurrying around as they prepared for a ceremony, but she wasn't sold on the place just yet.

"Well this is nice looking," Linc said as they climbed out of his truck. He met her in front of the truck and again laced his fingers in between hers. Brigid wasn't sure if it was for himself or to reassure her, but either way, it was welcome. Hand in hand, they strolled up to the office door.

Linc held the door for her as they stepped inside. There were potted plants of all shapes and sizes decorating the interior. A large counter ran along the back wall where a young woman was seated. The interior was finished in wood as well. The walls, floor, and even the counter, had been finished in a stained wood with a high glossy shine.

"How can I help you?" the lady behind the counter asked pleasantly.

"I'm Brigid Barnes, and this is Linc Olsen. We have an

appointment to look at the wedding venue," Brigid said politely as they walked over to the counter.

"Ah, yes. Let me go get Allison," she said before disappearing behind a door. Brigid looked up at the exposed beams and the trailing plants that were wrapped around them. A large skylight lit the room, making it feel natural inside the man-made space.

"Hello, I'm Allison Smith. It's nice to meet you," a woman said as she stepped through the doorway. Her blunt, shoulder-length blonde hair had streaks of gray in it. Her glasses were perched on the end of her nose. After shaking their hands, she slid the glasses up into her hair. "It's always a joy to meet couples who are planning their wedding. Such a wonderful occasion," she said with a warm smile which spread across her face.

"Thank you," Linc said. "We're happy to be here."

"Well, let's go look at the location, shall we?" she asked. Leading them to a side door, she held it open for them as they stepped out into the fresh air.

While they were walking, Allison listed all of the interesting facts about the nature reserve, but Brigid wasn't particularly interested in them.

Instead, she tried to imagine her guests coming here for the ceremony. What it would feel like to be there on her big day? She struggled to envision it. She could imagine a wedding taking place here at the nature reserve, but she wasn't sure she could see her wedding taking place here.

"It's a beautiful place," Linc said beside her. "I can't believe I haven't visited before now."

Brigid wasn't listening to Allison's response. The sinking feeling that Holly was right continued to nag her. She agreed with Linc that it was beautiful. Brigid could tell that in a few weeks the place would be even more beautiful, when it was alive with color. Even now, there were tiny buds on many of the plants with glimpses of color peeking out.

Superficially, the place was gorgeous. The native plants were all lovingly tended and cared for. There was wildlife that could be seen in the distance, blending in with their surroundings. Brigid wanted nothing more than to feel like this was the place she would ultimately select, but the closer they got to the spot where the actual ceremony would be conducted, the more certain she was that this wasn't for her.

Finally, they rounded a corner and Alison told them this was the location where they would take their vows. There was a nice open area with a small creek running through it. A gazebo was set at one end, raised so that everyone who gathered around it would have an excellent view of the wedding couple. It was all very lovely, but not what Brigid had hoped for. It still felt very formal and staged, not at all what she was envisioning in her mind.

"I'll let you two take a look around," Alison said. "Please, take your time. You don't even need to decide today. We aren't expecting any other weddings for the time you mentioned, so our schedule is currently wide open for this location. I wouldn't wait too long if you do choose us, however. You never know who may call." She shook each of their hands before leaving them so they could talk privately to each other.

"Well, what do you think?" Linc asked. "Is it what you had in mind?"

"Honestly? No," Brigid admitted. She could just hear Holly telling her she was right. "It's not exactly what I imagined."

"Are you sure?" Linc asked. "It's very pretty, and it will look even better once everything fills out. We could get married with deer strolling around behind us," he said as he pulled her close and wrapped his arms around her.

Brigid imagined a wedding ceremony being held in the nature

reserve, but as much as she tried, she could not see it as the place where she wanted Linc and her to say their vows.

She shook her head and sighed. "Nope. I'm sorry, but I just don't feel it. I want it to be less formal than this." She looked around and saw that some of the nearby flowers were starting to bloom. The natural beauty was a bit forced for her. It was in the planted flower beds and the way everything was arranged so perfectly. It wasn't natural and free-flowing.

"That's okay. At least we can rule it out," Linc said as he released her. He leaned over and picked an early blooming flower and tucked it in her hair.

"Linc! I don't think you're supposed to pick flowers in a nature reserve," Brigid said, shocked.

"Probably not, but it's not nearly as beautiful as you are," he said kissing her forehead. "So, you don't want to see anything else here?"

Brigid paused, tapping her fingernail on her front teeth. "Nope," she finally said. "It's just not our place, but we might as well take a walk around the loop trail and make it worth the trip," she said grinning. She couldn't believe how incredibly lucky she was to have a man who was so understanding and willing to let her take the lead. The fact that he was perfectly happy to just turn around and go home, because she said so, was quite touching to her.

"As you wish," he said as he held out his arm. They slowly walked along the trail, pointing out the cute little animals to each other as they went. Together, they laughed and enjoyed themselves before finally ending up back at the main office.

Brigid had grown quiet as they walked back to the truck.

"What's wrong, Brigid?" Linc asked as he opened her door.

"What if I can't decide? We wanted a late May wedding, but if I can't pick a place to have it…," she let her sentence trail off.

"It will all work out, you'll see," Linc said. "The more you stress, the harder it's going to seem. Just have faith, Brigid. You'll find the right place."

"You think?" she asked as she climbed up into her seat and looked at Linc, concern showing on her face.

"I know," Linc said confidently before shutting her door.

As he walked around to the driver's side of the truck, she tried to embody the confidence he had that everything would work out in the end. She was so used to planning and analyzing, that going with the flow was a foreign thing for her, but if other people could do it, so could she. Leaning back in the seat she took a deep breath and for just a moment, allowed herself to believe it would all work out.

CHAPTER THREE

"I have some work I need to finish today, but let's have dinner tonight. Okay with you?" Linc said as he pulled into Brigid's driveway.

"That sounds great. Your house or mine?" she asked as she collected her things. Her purse was on the floor by her feet, and she'd tucked her discarded jacket behind her.

"Why don't you come to my place? Bring Holly if she's not busy, but if she is, I won't be offended." Linc gave Brigid a wink and she laughed.

"I'll see what she's got going on. Talk to you later. Love you," she said as she leaned across the truck seat and kissed him.

Linc returned the kiss, nibbling on her lip slightly before leaning back. "Looking forward to it. Love you, too," he grinned.

As she got out of his truck, she heard her phone chime. Digging in her purse she saw it was her sister.

Busy? was all the text message said.

Nope. What do you need? she sent back. Walking towards her house, her sister quickly responded.

I could use a soda. Can you bring me one?

She sent back a thumbs up emoji. Pausing, Brigid thought about going inside the house for a moment, but decided that probably wasn't a good idea. Jett had a habit of thinking he needed to come in from outside as soon as someone came home. If she went in, he'd start scratching at the back door. She already felt sorry for the door from the other times he'd scratched at it. Big paws meant big claws, and he was well into the process of ruining the door.

Instead, she decided to leave without going inside. She climbed into her car, figuring she could finish proofreading the novel she'd been working on later. Anyway, there was no real need to go inside. She could tell Holly still wasn't home, because her bike wasn't in its usual place. Normally, she'd lock it up on the porch, but there was no sign of it.

It'd be nice to talk with Fiona about my wedding plans, she thought. She'd been so busy with work recently that she hadn't had a chance to visit with her sister as much as she'd like. Maybe a little sister time was exactly what she needed. Fiona was so into fashion and everything that was in style, she'd probably have some suggestions on how to get the wedding ball rolling.

As she pulled out of her driveway, she thought about all the things she still needed to decide. She needed a location, a cake, a dress, and a bouquet for starters. Everything beyond that was just icing on the cake, so to speak. She didn't want to go overboard and spend a lot of money on the ceremony. Linc and Brigid had decided that any money they saved by not going overboard on the wedding would go directly towards their honeymoon fund. To her, that was a much more worthwhile expense. She'd always thought it was a lot better to spend money on experiences rather than on things.

Brigid made a quick stop at the gas station and picked up Fiona's favorite soda before continuing on to the bookstore. Once inside, she heard her sister and another familiar voice laughing.

"Missy!" Brigid exclaimed as she entered. "I didn't realize you'd be here." She gave her friend a hug as they greeted each other.

"It's been so long since I've sat down with a good book, I came to visit your sister," she said. "Now that the holidays are over, I can take a little time to read."

"Good for you. You've had a lot going on the past few months," Fiona said. She turned to Brigid and said, "Thanks, Sis. I needed some liquid refreshment." She twisted the cap off the soda and took a big drink.

"I'd say so," Brigid chuckled. She turned to Missy, "Don't you have a lot to do to get ready for Easter?" Brigid asked as they moved over to the armchairs situated nearby and sat down. Missy was sipping a cup of coffee, her hands wrapped around the mug, as if they were cold.

"Yes, but it's not quite like the holidays. With all the needy families the church helps, I have a lot to keep track of. I'm always worried I'll forget someone or something," Missy said.

Fiona waved away the woman's concerns. "Girl, you are one of the most organized people I know. You couldn't forget something if you tried."

"I wish I was as sure of that as you are," Missy said nervously. "I swear, every year it's something new. We coordinate so much, but there are always those who are in need. Enough about me," she said waving her arms in front of her as if she were clearing the air. "How's the wedding planning coming along?" she asked as she turned her focus on Brigid.

"Terrible," Brigid said. "Linc and I just got back from checking out the nature reserve when I got Fiona's message."

"I've heard it's quite lovely," Missy said softly.

"It is," Brigid said. "It's wonderful, but it's just not the place I'm looking for. I have this image in my mind, but everywhere we go it just doesn't seem right. To tell you the truth, I'm starting to get worried," she admitted.

"Why?" Fiona asked. "There's nothing wrong with being a little picky about where you want to get married. I think every bride is. It will happen. Quit worrying about it."

"That's what everyone seems to think, but I'm not so sure. I wish I could find the perfect location for the wedding. That would make me feel a lot better. I think everything else would fall in place after that." Brigid sighed. "Maybe I should tell Linc I want to do it at the courthouse and be done with it."

"You know you don't want that," Fiona chastised. "You're just overwhelmed. Every time you check out a new location, and it isn't what you want, you say the same thing."

"You know you're always welcome at our church," Missy said softly.

"I know, Missy," Brigid said. "And I really appreciate that, but Linc and I really want to do something outdoors. Both of us were married in a church the first time. We agreed we wanted to do it differently this time."

"Well," Missy said, "the offer still stands."

"I'm incredibly grateful for that. Thanks," Brigid said. "It's wonderful to know you're so supportive." She reached over and touched her friend's arm tenderly.

"So what's the problem?" Fiona asked. "What are you looking for in a location? What is it that everywhere you've looked seems to be lacking something?"

"I'm not sure," Brigid said. "My thought was to find somewhere that meant something to Linc and me. Yet I also want something that doesn't feel fussy and complicated. The best way to describe it is to compare it to a date. So instead of having a fancy dinner at an expensive restaurant, I would rather have an evening on the couch under a comfy blanket. I don't really want somewhere just because it's pretty." She sighed. "I'm probably not making any sense."

"No, it does make sense," Missy said. "You want something that reflects you two as a couple. You guys aren't fancy and flashy. You're centered, grounded, and loving. Where did you two meet?" Missy asked, leaning forward as she crossed her legs.

"On my front porch, actually. Kind of in my yard," Brigid said with a smile as she remembered the first time she'd seen Linc.

"I don't think I've heard this story," Missy said as she settled into her chair.

"There's not a lot to it," Brigid began. "He noticed I was moving in and came over to introduce himself. We shared a bottle of wine and got to know one another. He'd known the people who had lived there previously, mainly because of Jett."

"Why's that?" Missy asked.

"Jett actually belonged to the couple I bought the house from. They were downsizing and couldn't take him to where they were moving. I'd always wanted a dog, so I said I'd take him." She smiled, remembering when she'd first seen the big lug. "Jett always liked to take off for Linc's yard before I moved in and agreed to keep him," she explained.

"So you guys really did meet in your yard?" Missy questioned.

"Oh, your yard would be perfect," Fiona cooed. Missy nodded.

"Nobody gets married in their front yard," Brigid scoffed.

"Actually, you'd be surprised," Fiona said. "It's been done a number of times."

"Really?" Brigid asked. Her mind began to work on the logistics of such a proposition.

"Sure, after all, it's your wedding. You can do whatever you want." Fiona took another big drink and finished the bottle of soda. She turned and tossed it in the trash. "Oh, but I know who you definitely have to have make your bouquet."

"Who?" Brigid asked.

"Olivia Ford. She owns Ford's Flowers over on the square. I've seen some of her arrangements, and they are amazing," Fiona gushed.

"Isn't that where old man Duane used to have his flower shop?" Brigid asked.

Fiona nodded. "Yep. She bought it from him. She's been there for a little while now and has made quite a name for herself."

Missy nodded. "I agree. I've seen some of her work for weddings that have been held at our church. Everything she does is beautiful and just a bit different from the usual. I can't put my finger on why, but it is."

"Okay," Brigid said as she pulled out her phone. "I'll call her and talk to her." She began searching for the number before saving it to her phone.

"You'll probably have to make an appointment," Missy said. "She's usually pretty busy."

Brigid nodded. "I will." It sounded to her as though Olivia would be the best person for the job. Maybe having a florist picked out to do her bouquet would help her finalize a few other choices as well.

"What about your dress? Have you looked at any yet?" Fiona asked. Brigid wasn't surprised her sister's mind was on the dress. It was her favorite part of any wedding. She even liked to watch the television show where the women picked out their wedding dresses.

As far as Brigid knew, she'd seen every episode.

"No, but I have been thinking about it. I've looked online, and that's a start," Brigid said softly.

"Dang, girl. You're doing what?" Fiona asked incredulously.

Brigid's forehead bunched up. "I looked at ideas online."

"Oh, no, no, no," Fiona said. "Take me dress shopping with you, and we'll get something picked out for the wedding."

"I don't know, Fiona. Our styles aren't exactly the same," Brigid said as she tried to tiptoe around the subject. Her sister tended to be a bit more flamboyant and colorful, while Brigid preferred things that were a little more sedate and conservative.

"Yeah, because I have some style. Come on, it'll be fun." Fiona folded her hands and got down on her knees in front of her sister. "Please? I promise we'll have a good time."

"Oh, alright," Brigid said, giving in. "Besides, I need to ask you two something. Missy, I'd love it if you could be one of my bridesmaids."

Missy broke into a wide grin. "You know I will. How exciting!" she squealed.

"Good," Brigid said smiling. "And Fiona? I want you to be my matron-of-honor."

"Absolutely!" Fiona said clapping. "That means I get to have some fun."

"Don't get too out of control. I plan on asking Holly to be a bridesmaid, but I haven't mentioned anything to her yet."

"She'll be so excited," Fiona said. "She's already talking about the wedding all the time."

"Has she? Well, she may be a bit more distracted now," Brigid said softly.

"Why? What happened?" Both women asked.

"Apparently, her aunt in Missouri contacted her. She's asked Holly to come to Missouri and stay with her family sometime this summer. We're thinking she should go when Linc and I go on our honeymoon," Brigid shrugged.

"That sounds like a great opportunity to get to know her family," Fiona said. "Why do you look so glum?"

At first, Brigid debated whether or not she should tell them how she felt about it. After all, it was pretty selfish of her to think that way. In the end, she realized Missy and Fiona were two people she could trust, no matter what. They wouldn't judge her or dismiss her feelings. If anything, they'd probably help her see she was being ridiculous.

"I'm afraid she might not want to stay with me anymore. Going somewhere where she's surrounded by her real family, people she's biologically related to, may change her mind. The truth is, I've gotten so used to having her around, I can't imagine my life without her," Brigid admitted.

Fiona made a harrumphing noise. "Don't worry about it, Brigid. She loves you. Even if she did want to stay there, she'd never just skip out of your life. You could still email, text, call, or whatever," she pointed out. "You mean a lot more to her than you realize."

"I know," Brigid sighed. "I just don't like the thought of her not being here." Truth be told, her heart felt heavy just thinking about it.

"Why don't you cross that bridge when you get there?" Missy said as she took Brigid's hand. "There's no use worrying about something that may never happen. Let Holly go and enjoy herself. If she brings it up when she comes back, you can deal with it then. Until that happens, I think you have enough on your plate right now without adding something more to it."

Brigid nodded. "You're right." Taking a deep breath, she checked the time on her watch. "I better go if I'm going to make that call. Plus, I still need to run by the store and pick up a few things. I'll talk to you two soon, so we can make plans to go dress shopping together." She stood up and gave each of them a big hug.

When she stepped out of the bookstore, Brigid felt as though a weight had been lifted from her shoulders. The sun seemed just a little brighter and the air a bit fresher. *Maybe things are going to turn out okay after all,* she thought.

CHAPTER FOUR

Brigid and Holly arrived at Linc's house that evening for dinner shortly after 6:00. Holly was planning on going to a friend's house for dinner, but once she heard Linc would be cooking, she changed her plans.

"It's not that you aren't a great cook, Brigid," she explained. "But when Linc makes something, it's out of this world." Holly rubbed her hands together in anticipation.

"I agree," Brigid said, nodding eagerly. "He does an amazing job. You know, I could have brought home leftovers for you, and then you could have gone to your friend's."

"That's okay," Holly said. "I'd rather spend time with you guys tonight. Feels like forever since we've come over here." Holly stepped forward and knocked on Linc's front door.

"Come in!" They heard Linc yell from somewhere deep inside the house. "The door's unlocked."

Pushing the door open, they heard the sound of food sizzling, and the tantalizing aroma of whatever he was cooking surrounded them.

"I'm glad we didn't bring Jett this time," Brigid mentioned. "He would have gone nuts over this smell."

Holly nodded. "He wouldn't be the only one. I'm also going nuts over this smell."

They found Linc sliding food onto plates and whistling as he worked. Steam was rising from the pans and music was playing softly in the background.

"What are you making?" Holly asked as she walked in and leaned over the stove. She took a deep breath, closing her eyes, savoring the scent.

"Scallops with an alfredo sauce over linguini, garlic bread, and a salad," he said. "Will that work for you?"

"It will more than work for me," Holly said. "It smells amazing!" She began to help Linc serve dinner, while Brigid sat down at the table. When he wasn't looking, she dipped a spoon in and took a taste. She turned and mouthed "Oh my goodness!" to Brigid, who smiled at her enthusiasm.

"Holly has some exciting news," Brigid said as they served dinner.

"Oh? What's that?" Linc asked, turning to Holly.

"My aunt from Missouri got in touch with me. She wants me to visit her and her family this summer. Brigid and I were talking and thought maybe I could go when you guys leave on your honeymoon," she said as she sat down at the table.

"That sounds exciting," Linc said, noticing that Brigid didn't look quite as thrilled as Holly. Whenever Holly looked at Brigid, her face would brighten, but when she didn't think anyone was looking, Brigid's face would fall.

"I wasn't so sure at first," Holly admitted. "But Brigid said she thought it would be a good idea, so I agreed. Now that my aunt, Katie is her name, has sent me pictures of her place and my cousins, I have to admit I'm kind of excited. I don't know why, but I expected them to live in a small town, too, but they don't."

"Where do they live?" Linc asked.

Holly scrunched up her face as she tried to remember. "I can't think of it offhand. I'll have to check out her email when we get home. I'm really starting to look forward to it, though," she said excitedly.

"That's good," Linc said as they began to eat. "And what about you Brigid? How do you feel about it?"

Brigid looked up, somewhat surprised he'd asked that question. "If Holly's happy, I'm happy," she said softly as she took Holly's hand in hers.

Holly didn't notice that Brigid seemed distracted, and she simply smiled. "I'll find out more soon and when I do, I'll let you know," she said. "So how did the nature reserve go?"

"You were right," Brigid sighed. "I didn't go for it."

"Told you so," Holly said, as she put a big bite of the scallops and pasta in her mouth. "Don't worry, you'll figure it out."

"I hope so," Brigid said. "But I have begun to take some steps for the wedding. I have a meeting with the owner of Ford's Flowers tomorrow morning. Fiona recommended her."

"You're going to have Olivia do your flowers?" Holly gasped.

"I may. Why? Do you know her?" Brigid asked.

"No, but I've heard she's awesome. When it's prom time, she makes unique corsages and boutonnieres for people. She doesn't do the standard baby's breath and stuff like that. She changes it up for each person. I've seen pictures of what she's created, and they're way cool," she said, nodding her approval.

"You hear that, Brigid? She does cool work," Linc said as he teased Holly.

"Oh, knock it off," she said laughing loudly. She and Linc had started teasing each other recently. It made Brigid smile and distracted her from all the stressors of the day.

"Fiona brought something up that I've been thinking about," Brigid said, interrupting their teasing.

"What's that?" Linc said, turning towards her.

"She suggested having our wedding where we first met," Brigid said.

"We met in your front yard. On your front porch," Linc said with a questioning look on his face.

"I think that would really be neat. You could have it in that big space between your houses," Holly said with a smile.

"I've been considering it," Brigid said. "But I don't know if that would be a little too informal for a wedding," she admitted. She felt as though she was going back and forth. First, she was worried about the place being too formal. Now, she was worried about the place being too informal.

"I don't think so, but just like I've told you before, I'm happy if you're happy. We could get married in the back of a semi-trailer, and I wouldn't care," Linc chuckled.

"Ew, no," Holly said wrinkling her nose. "I'd care. That's not a bad idea, though, Brigid. Seriously, think about it. You could rent some chairs and tables and set up a nice little area. Maybe get one of those big tent things if you wanted to."

Brigid tried to imagine how it would look. There was definitely enough space for it, but she wasn't sure about the reception. She told Linc her concerns.

"We could have the ceremony there and do the reception somewhere else. Or, we could rent one of those tents like Holly said?" he suggested.

Suddenly, the whole thing came to her. Brigid could imagine an archway built from branches they could find in the woods behind their houses. The background of their nuptials would be the stunning view of the forest behind the house. If they positioned it just right, they could even backdrop it with the creek that ran in the distance.

"I think I like it," she said so quietly she wasn't sure if anyone heard her until Holly spoke.

"Really?" Holly said. "Is that what you want to do?"

"Do you like the idea?" Brigid asked, turning towards Holly.

"Brigid, first, it doesn't matter what I think, it's about what you think. Second, I do like it. The view is amazing, and it would be completely different from everyone else's wedding. Nobody else has or could be married there," she pointed out.

Linc nodded. "I like it, too, but only if you do."

They quietly began to eat while Brigid continued to think. Linc and Holly began talking about their favorite television shows while Brigid started thinking seriously about having the wedding in the front yard. They could fit in pretty much everyone they'd want to invite. There wasn't a size limitation, and it was certainly a unique venue. It met all of the criteria she'd mentally outlined when she was trying to decide what she wanted in a location.

She began to smile as things started to come together in her mind. *That was why I couldn't find the place I wanted,* she thought. *It was right under my nose the whole time. What better place to be married than the location where Linc and I first laid eyes on each other?*

Brigid felt an imaginary weight lifted off her chest. Now, she could plan her wedding. She was free to pick any date she wanted, and it didn't have to be one that some other location had available. There was no one else she needed to check with. The decision had been made.

"I think that's where we're going to be married," she finally said.

Both Linc and Holly looked at her surprised. "Good," Holly said. "Now that you've made the decision, you can stop stressing so much and chill out a little."

The conversation changed to Linc's work and then school for Holly. Brigid listened, but her attention was more focused on dreaming up ideas for her big day.

"I've got some homework I need to do, so if it's okay with you guys, I'm going to let you have some alone time," Holly said when they'd finished dinner. She stood up and collected Brigid and Linc's plates, carrying them to the sink.

"That's fine," Brigid said as Holly returned and leaned over her, giving the older woman a hug. "Make sure you let Jett back in when you get home."

"I will," Holly said as she hugged Linc. "Don't have too much fun while I'm gone," she said with a wink.

Linc raised his hands. "Wouldn't dream of it, boss." He waited until Holly left before standing up and changing the song on his iPhone. Turning it up, he smiled at her. "Remember this?" he asked as he took Brigid's hand.

She smiled. "Of course I do," she said. "Our first dance."

"That's right," he said as he pulled her into his arms and began to slowly dance with her, swaying back and forth. "So, what has you so distracted? You hardly said a word during dinner."

"The wedding, for one thing. I definitely think we'll do it in the yard," she said. "It's intimate and means something to us."

Linc nodded. "Sounds great, but what else is bothering you?"

"What do you mean?" Brigid asked, looking away.

"I know that's not all of it, so come out with it," he said forcing her to look at him.

"I'm just worried Holly will like this Aunt Katie's place more than mine and want to stay there permanently," she admitted.

"I don't think that's possible," Linc said easily.

"You don't?" Brigid asked.

He shook his head. "There's no way she could be nearly as cool as you. Holly loves you. You know that. Don't worry so much about the things you can't control. Let them happen the way they're meant to. You've already made a tremendous difference in Holly's life, and she knows that. She's like a new person. She's much more confident now and holds her head high. You're the one who encouraged her and allowed her to do that," Linc said as he pulled Brigid closer until their bodies were pressed tightly together.

"I guess you're right," Brigid admitted. "I just worry about her."

"I think that's what being a parent is all about, and that's true as it applies to you even though you are only an informal or semi-adopted parent," Linc said gently. "You just have to hope you did a good enough job with the time you had." He looked down at her and said, "She's a good kid. Don't worry so much."

"Okay," Brigid said. "I'll try."

"Good, now I think we should have dessert," he said smiling his boyish grin.

"Oh? You made dessert?" she asked.

"No, but we will," he said with a wink as he pulled her toward the bedroom.

CHAPTER FIVE

Brigid and Mike were still at the flower shop talking with concern about Olivia, Mike's wife, suddenly missing, when Mike said, "I can't believe something like this happened in our small town. How could my wife just disappear into thin air? It makes no sense."

"Don't worry, Sheriff Davis will figure out what happened to her," Brigid said reassuringly. She may have been distracted and tired this morning but now she was fully awake. While she was used to people being murdered, there was something eerie about a young woman simply disappearing. Of course, with time they should have some leads, but for now, it was as if she'd disappeared into thin air.

"I really want you to help, Brigid," Mike said. "I know it's not a murder, at least I pray it isn't, but Corey's told me how good you are at getting to the bottom of things."

Brigid shrugged. "I think it has more to do with the fact I'm not the police. Many people freeze up around someone in uniform. I'm not in law enforcement, so I believe they feel more comfortable talking with someone like me."

"I'm going to call Corey and let him know that I asked you to help," Mike said as he moved behind the counter. He pulled out his phone and began to punch in the numbers as Brigid started piecing together what she knew.

Olivia had gone to the market earlier this morning by herself, and in a small town like Cottonwood Springs, she'd probably spoken to a few people while she was there. Brigid began to formulate a plan while Mike was speaking to Sheriff Davis.

"Corey asked if you could meet him over at the grocery store in a few minutes. I said you could because if Olivia was here, you'd be spending time here, so I figured you'd already set aside some time," Mike said after he ended the call.

"Not a problem," Brigid said. "I gave you my cell number. Let me know if you think of anything relevant. I'll keep you posted, and I'm sure Sheriff Davis will too. Try not to worry, Mike. We'll do everything we can to get her back home quickly and safely," Brigid said reassuringly. She wasn't quite sure how they were going to do that, but she wasn't going to tell him that. More than likely, he already knew.

"Thank you," he said. "I'm worried sick. I feel like I should be doing something, but my mind won't calm down enough for me to think," he admitted.

"Just try to relax," she said. "Go stay with friends or family if you need to. Being alone is one of the worst things you can do. Your mind has too much free time that way." Brigid couldn't imagine what the poor man must be going through. How would she feel if Linc or Holly disappeared? There would be no consoling her.

"I better go meet Corey," Brigid said, after she was certain Mike was okay. "I'll let you know what I find out later today."

Mike nodded and she went out the door. Brigid had watched enough true crime shows to know that even though this wasn't a murder, time was of the essence. Would someone come forward asking for a ransom for Olivia's return? It was always possible, but Brigid had a feeling her disappearance wasn't that simple.

It wasn't like Olivia was some billionaire's daughter. No, she was just a small business owner who was trying to make a living and help pay the monthly expenses. More than likely, if someone had kidnapped Olivia, this person had a much worse motive in mind than money. They had to find her before it was too late.

A few minutes later Brigid arrived at the grocery store. Sheriff Davis' deputies were combing over what she assumed was Olivia's car, a dark blue sedan. As she walked across the parking lot, Sheriff Davis stepped out of the front door of the store, the doors squeaking as they slid open.

"I'm glad you're here," he said. "Think this is gonna' be an 'all hands on deck' sorta' situation." He took his brown hat off and ran his hand through his thick dark hair.

"Happy to help if I can," Brigid said. "What do you know so far?"

"Not much. Follow me," he said as he turned and walked back into the store. "The manager's bringin' up the footage from the security cameras right now. It took some time before anyone actually realized somethin' was wrong, so we'll have to track a few people down. Plan is, we see who was here and what happened outside. Then, we talk to everyone to make sure she didn't stage this herself. Ya' know, get a feel for her mindset and all."

Brigid nodded. "That makes sense. We can also find out if she gave away any clues that she knew something would happen."

"Right. Hopefully, the video from the security camera will provide us with somethin' to help us find whoever did this, and more importantly, find our victim before somethin' really bad happens to her. People usually see more than they realize, so we're gonna' have to talk to anyone who saw or talked to her while she was here at the store. Good thing it was so early in the day, cuz' there weren't many people here at that time, Sheriff Davis said with a determined look on his face.

"Mike Ford's one of my best friends," he finally admitted. "I can't imagine what he's goin' through."

"We'll find her," Brigid said. "I'm confident of it."

"I know we will," he said. "Guess I'm more worried about what she may be goin' through right now. I've heard about these human traffickin' people showin' up in places besides big cities. It seems like it was only a matter of time before they came to realize how relaxed we small town folks are." He shook his head with worry. "I jes' hope that ain't the case. These guys move fast. I've heard once they get across the border, it's almost impossible to catch 'em."

"Then we have to be quick," Brigid said determinedly. "If that's the case, we can't give them that option."

"Yeah, yer' right," he said, but Brigid could see the tension in his shoulders. He was taking this crime to heart, and she couldn't blame him. As the sheriff, more than likely he felt as though he had to protect everyone in his jurisdiction. Having someone disappear was certainly unnerving. What if whoever had done it didn't stop with Olivia?

They walked to the back of the store and stopped just outside a door marked "Security." Sheriff Davis opened the door for Brigid, and they stepped inside. The office was fairly plain with white walls and an off-white tile floor. An older woman with chin-length salt and pepper hair was in the room sitting in front of a computer screen.

"It's ready to go. This is the parking lot footage," she said as they walked over and stood behind the desk where she was sitting.

"Go ahead and play it," Sheriff Davis said.

They watched the screen as a woman Brigid assumed was Olivia moved to the passenger side of her car. She opened the door and put her shopping bags inside as a white van pulled up next to her, obstructing the security camera's view. A few moments later the van quickly pulled away, and Olivia was gone.

"Either they knew the camera was there or these guys got dumb luck," Sheriff Davis said. "Not only could we not see what was happenin', there's no way to see the license plate, and their windows are tinted so dark ya' can't even see the driver." He sighed. "At this point, all we got is a vehicle description."

"I've got the store footage queued up whenever you're ready," the woman said.

"Go ahead," Sheriff Davis instructed.

She started it and they saw the inside of the store displayed on the screen. They watched as Olivia entered and picked up a hand-held grocery basket. Slowly, she moved among the aisles and then stopped when she started talking to someone.

"That looks like MaryAnn Thompson," Brigid said as they watched the two women chat for a few moments before Olivia moved on down the aisle.

Sheriff Davis wrote her name in his notebook. "Yer' right. I remember her from when Holly's mother was murdered. Good eye, Brigid."

Olivia continued walking down the aisle. She picked up a bag of chips before she stopped to talk to Eve Sterling.

"That's Eve Sterling," Sheriff Davis said as he began to write in his notebook. They fell silent again as Oliva turned down another aisle and continued on. She looked as though she was getting ready to leave when she paused.

"And that's Missy," Brigid said. There was no mistaking her friend.

"From the church? Right?" Sheriff Davis asked.

Brigid nodded as they watched Oliva move to the checkout counter and start talking with the cashier.

"Looks like we got four people that we need to talk to," Sheriff Davis said. He looked up at Brigid, "Ya' think ya' can handle that part while my people search her car and parkin' lot for evidence?"

"Not a problem," Brigid said.

Sheriff Davis tore the list out of his notebook and handed it to Brigid. "Here's the list. Why don't'cha start with the cashier, since she's still here. I'm gonna' do some callin' around and see what I can find out. If there are kidnappers or human traffickers in the area, they've probably been to other places and maybe somebody knows somethin'. No sense tryin' to reinvent the wheel."

Brigid nodded. It looked like it was time for her to start questioning people again. She wasn't sure if it was a good thing that she was beginning to feel comfortable doing it, but she was more than happy to help. There was no way she could just sit this one out and pray for the best.

CHAPTER SIX

"Can you tell me where I could find the cashier who was working when Olivia checked out earlier this morning?" Brigid asked the manager.

"She should be in the break room. Step outside, turn left, and go through the swinging double doors. The break room is on your right," the woman said.

Brigid thanked her and stepped out of the office. There were a few customers milling about, oblivious to what had happened there earlier that morning. Could it be that human trafficking had made its way to their small town? She didn't like the thought of that.

So many people in town left their front doors unlocked because they'd grown up that way. They felt safe, even with their doors unlocked. That might be about to change given the shocking circumstances of what had happened to Oliva.

There was no such thing as a stranger for many of the town's residents. Brigid's stomach began to burn at the thought of how so many people could be susceptible because of their innocent faith in people. There was a good chance Olivia was just being friendly to the people in the van, and she wound up being missing because of it.

Following the manager's directions, Brigid found the break room.

A young woman, who looked to be about nineteen, was sitting at the table in a folding chair. Brigid recognized her from the video she and the sheriff had just watched, but now the woman looked uneasy.

"Excuse me," Brigid said as she entered the room. "My name's Brigid. I came to talk to you about the woman who disappeared this morning."

The girl nodded, her black hair hanging down in her eyes. When she brushed it away, it was obvious she'd been crying.

"Are you okay?" Brigid asked.

"I'm fine," the girl said. "I just feel terrible."

Brigid noticed the name tag on her shirt indicated that her name was Cadence. "It's not your fault, Cadence. Sometimes these things just happen."

"I know. It's just, I wish when I heard the van peel out that I would have gone outside and gotten their license plate number or something. Instead I just continued to read my magazine," she sniffled.

"I'm afraid hindsight is always 20/20," Brigid said as she consoled her. "Why don't you tell me everything you can remember? Was there anyone in the store who seemed out of the ordinary?"

"Not really," Cadence said. "I didn't notice anyone come in the store that I hadn't seen before. Just the regulars. With the big windows out front, I try to watch the parking lot, but I don't remember seeing that van pull in. I only noticed it when it took off."

Brigid pulled the notebook she'd started keeping in her purse out and began to write in it. "What did Olivia talk about while she was checking out? Anything specific?"

Cadence shook her head. "Not really. She talked about the weather and how nice it was that it was warming up. She mentioned maybe going for a walk this evening if it stayed nice."

Nodding, Brigid made a note. "She didn't seem worried or stressed or anything like that?"

"Not at all," the girl said. "If anything, she seemed happy. Chipper, even. Like, too happy for that early in the morning," she chuckled, then her face grew somber as she asked, "You don't think this is like those other people, do you?"

"What do you mean?" Brigid asked.

"Some of my friends were talking about it last week. There's a handful of people around the area that have gone missing lately. Mostly women, but there were a couple of young men, also. Almost all of their cars were found, but there's no trace of them." Cadence shivered. "To be honest, it kind of freaks me out."

Brigid tried to hide her growing concern. She hadn't been on social media or anything like that for some time, so she hadn't heard anything about this. If it was a growing problem, maybe she shouldn't be letting Holly ride her bike everywhere. She knew Holly would balk at her worries, but if this sort of thing had found its way to Cottonwood Springs, it was time to make some changes.

"I really don't know," Brigid said honestly. "I certainly hope not. Is there anything you can tell me about the van?" With it being the only clue they had at the present, Brigid was hoping to get better details about it.

"Let me think," the girl began. "Well, it was white, pretty basic if you ask me. Almost too basic, now that I think about it. There weren't any side windows, and the one up front on the passenger side, at least the one I saw, was tinted pretty dark. All I could see was a guy's arm."

"Are you sure it was a guy?" Brigid asked.

"I can't say for certain, no, but something about it seemed like a man. Maybe the way he was driving or something. I'm not sure. Or the size of the arm maybe? It just seemed like a man's arm to me."

Brigid nodded. "Anything else stand out about it?"

Cadence thought for a moment more. "I think the back windows may have had something just inside them, like maybe some sort of wire or screen. I think they may have been tinted, too. Do you know what I'm talking about?"

Brigid nodded. "I think so. Almost like that cage stuff they put in the back of service vehicles? Like to protect the windows or something?"

"Yeah, it was kind of like that," Cadence said. "That's all I can think of for now."

Brigid nodded. "You've been a big help. Try not to worry too much. I'm sure we'll find her." She patted the girl's hand reassuringly.

"Do you think we should all be more careful now?" she asked, her eyes wide. "Like, should we go places in pairs and stuff?"

"I never think it's a bad idea to err on the side of caution," Brigid said carefully. "After all, you just never know what could happen. If you have someone with you, at least you're a bit safer." She didn't want to worry the girl, but she also didn't want to blow off her concerns. It was always better to be safe than sorry.

Cadence nodded. "Yeah, you're right. Good luck," she said.

Brigid stood up and left the break room. Hurrying through the store, she saw Sheriff Davis leaving the store and heading towards the parking lot. She followed him.

"Sheriff Davis," she said as she hurried to joined him outside.

"Get anythin' from the cashier?" he asked.

"Not a whole lot. So far it seems like we're looking for a service type vehicle with tinted windows. Kind of like one a cable or utility company would use."

"Yeah, that's what I was thinkin', too," he said, "jes' by the looks of it from that surveillance video."

"Is it true there are people going missing from nearby towns?" Brigid asked.

Sheriff Davis became quiet, almost as if he was having an internal debate with himself. It looked like he was going to give her a recited speech, but then he evidently thought better of it. "It's true. I haven't looked into those cases, since they ain't in my jurisdiction. Didn't want to mention it, but yeah, I've heard talk. It's all been in counties a little farther away until now. But it's lookin' that way. I haven't checked anywhere closer recently, but I have a feelin' when I start callin' around, I'll hear similar stories."

A chill ran through Brigid. "What are we going to do?"

"The only thing we can do," he said. "Focus on this case and hope we solve it. Ain't much anyone can do but try to piece things together. If you're the prayin' type, that wouldn't hurt, either."

Brigid nodded. "I'm going to see if I can talk to the other people on the list."

"Sounds like a plan, Brigid. Ya' let me know if you find out anythin'. Anythin' at all, ya' hear?"

"Absolutely," she said nodding. "You have my word."

"By the way, Brigid, try not to be a vigilante this time. Gives me migraines and more paperwork than I care to deal with," he said with a smirk.

"I'll do my best," Brigid said. Even as she gave him her word, she knew she'd do whatever was necessary.

CHAPTER SEVEN

Brigid was sitting in her car, trying to decide which one of the people who talked to Olivia at the grocery store earlier that morning she should start with when her phone rang. It was her sister, Fiona.

"Good morning," Fiona said enthusiastically.

"If you say so," Brigid mumbled as she looked over her list.

"What's up with you this morning, grumpy pants?" Fiona asked.

"Well, I had my appointment this morning to meet with Olivia from Ford's Flowers," Brigid began.

"Oh, dear, did it go badly?" Fiona asked. "Is she too busy to do a bouquet for you?"

"No, it's nothing like that. It seems she's disappeared," Brigid said as she sat back in her seat.

"What?" Fiona cried.

"Yep. She disappeared right out of the grocery store parking lot earlier this morning. I talked to her husband, Mike, and he asked me to help Sheriff Davis find her."

"What did Corey say?"

"He welcomed the help. He told me his department had their hands full processing the crime scene, and he asked me to talk to anyone who Olivia had spoken with at the store this morning," Brigid said with a sigh.

"I swear, you need to join the sheriff's department," Fiona joked. "I think you're conducting investigations about as often as they do."

"Yeah, but I don't want to have to write tickets. Of course, all I'd have to do is follow you around, but I'd need a new ticket book every week," Brigid teased.

"Hey, that's not funny," Fiona said seriously. "I'm calling because I heard there was a going-out-of-business sale at that formal dress shop over on the outskirts of town. I thought maybe we could head over there and see what they have," she suggested.

"Sure," Brigid said. "Why don't you call Missy and ask her to join us? I need to talk to her, anyway. Sheriff Davis wants me to question everyone who spoke to Olivia in the store this morning, and Missy was one of them. That will save me a trip, because I'll just talk to her when we go to the shop. By the way, did Holly show up for work?"

"She sure did. Why are you asking?" Fiona asked.

Brigid sighed deeply. "It's looks like Olivia going missing is not an isolated incident. Apparently, several other people have disappeared around here, or so I've heard. It could be nothing, or it could all be connected. I'd just feel better if she didn't ride her bike home."

"No problem. I'll start giving her a ride when I can. Until then, you find this creep. If anyone can do it, it's you," Fiona said confidently.

"I hope so. I don't like the idea there could be someone out there snatching women out of parking lots," Brigid said. "Freaks me out."

"Me, too," Fiona said softly. "Meet me at the bookstore around 3:00?

Missy, you, and me can all go together."

"Sounds good. See you then," Brigid said as she ended the call.

Brigid decided the first stop she'd make would be to visit MaryAnn Thompson. Now that she had the new baby, she'd probably be at home. She, along with Missy, would be the easiest ones to find. She started her car, pulled away from the grocery store, and headed towards MaryAnn's home.

Brigid hadn't seen MaryAnn in over a year. The last time she'd really spoken to her was when she was investigating the murder of Holly's mother. Her beautiful home hadn't changed. It was clearly still the most beautiful residence in Cottonwood Springs.

MaryAnn opened the front door in response to Brigid's knock . "Brigid Barnes, how good to see you. Come in," MaryAnn said, holding a little baby girl in her arms.

"How are you doing, MaryAnn?" Brigid asked as the women greeted each other. They'd seen each other in passing since then, a smile across the store, or a wave as they drove past one another, but other than that, they hadn't really talked since the murder investigation. "And this must be your baby girl. She's beautiful."

"Thanks. I'm doing wonderful. Much better than the last time we spoke. And yes, this is our little girl, Cameron. How's that young lady, Holly, doing?" she asked.

"Very well," Brigid said smiling politely.

Just then, MaryAnn's husband, Mark, walked up to them. He smiled at Brigid as he made faces at the little girl MaryAnn was holding. Her chubby little cheeks were rosy, and her hair had a bright red bow on it. She was grinning from ear to ear at the faces he was making at her.

"Did you eat that whole cookie?" he growled playfully, which only made the little girl squeal louder.

"How are you two coping with a baby?" Brigid asked.

"Exhausting," MaryAnn admitted. "But oddly satisfying. I've never been so happy and yet tired all at the same time," she laughed.

"I bet," said Brigid. "Apparently you're doing something right. It looks like she's a very happy baby."

"Thank you. Yes, she is," MaryAnn said. Mark took Cameron from MaryAnn and began to bounce her up and down as he made silly noises. He said a quick hello to Brigid and disappeared with his daughter. "So, what did you stop by for? Want to talk to us about getting a new bed or something from the furniture store? By the way, I heard that you're engaged. Congratulations!"

"Yes, I am," she said smiling. "But unfortunately, I'm not here for fun. Do you know Olivia Ford?"

"Of course. I just saw her this morning," MaryAnn said softly. "What's wrong?"

"It seems she's gone missing. It looks like someone snatched her right out of the parking lot at the grocery store this morning," Brigid informed her.

"You know, I thought something wasn't right," MaryAnn said, crossing her arms. "I knew she'd left the store before me, but I saw her car in the parking lot when I went out to my car. I didn't pay any attention to it. I thought maybe she was sitting in her car talking on the phone or looking at her email. I do remember noticing her car and thinking that was odd."

"According to what we know, shortly after she made it to her car a white van with tinted windows pulled up and blocked the grocery store's security camera. It seems they loaded her up and took off. The cashier heard their tires squeal when they left, but that's about all we have so far. I'm going around and talking to people who were at the store this morning to see if anyone noticed anything," Brigid said with a sigh.

"Wait a minute. Did you say a white van?" MaryAnn asked.

"Yes, why? Did you see something?" Brigid asked anxiously.

"Not really. It's just, as I was walking up to the store when I first got there, I noticed a white van. It was parked near the edge of the parking lot. I noticed someone inside, but whoever it was had a newspaper raised up in front of their face, as if they were reading it, so I couldn't really see who it was, but it looked like a man. He might have had dark hair, but I'm not sure." She thought for a moment before continuing, "The side windows appeared to be tinted, because they had a bluish color to them."

"Excellent," Brigid said as she took down a few notes, so that she'd be sure to remember and tell Sheriff Davis. "Can you think of anything else about the van? Where exactly was it parked?"

"You know that fence on the north side of the parking lot? It was backed into a parking spot over there. It's the closest one to the store, kind of tucked out of the way. Oh, I just remembered that the bumper was messed up. The grill, too. Like maybe they'd been in a traffic accident recently because there was quite a bit of front-end damage to the van."

"Great, that really helps, MaryAnn. The security camera didn't really catch much but the passenger side of the van, so we don't have a whole lot to go on." Brigid finished writing in her notebook what MaryAnn had told her. "Can you think of anything else?"

"No, I'm afraid not," she sighed. "I wish I'd paid more attention. If I'd known...,"

"I understand. Don't beat yourself up about it. There was no way you could have known at the time. Did Olivia say anything that stood out to you?" Brigid asked.

"Not that I recall. We spoke about Cameron, my daughter, and we chatted about last week's church service. Nothing too important," MaryAnn said shaking her head. "Sorry."

"No, this is good. Really. You've helped a lot. We think it's a kidnapping, but I want to make sure she didn't say something that might indicate otherwise. If you remember anything, please call the sheriff or me, okay?" Brigid asked softly.

While she was glad no one had been murdered this time, the thought of Olivia being in danger was stressful. She wasn't sure what was going on and just as importantly, if anyone else would be next on the disappearance list.

"I will. I hope you find her. She's such a good person. I can't imagine why anyone would want to take her."

"Right now, there's no way to know," Brigid said. Her imagination had already gone into overdrive. The only way she could focus was to put those thoughts away until she had time to deal with them.

MaryAnn nodded. "You're probably right. I'll be praying for her safe return. Hopefully she'll be found soon. Good luck in your search," she said.

"Thank you," Brigid said as she turned to leave. Once she was outside, she took her phone out of her pocket and dialed Sheriff Davis.

"Brigid, what have ya' found out?" he asked as he picked up her call.

"According to MaryAnn Thompson, a white van with front end damage to the bumper and grill, was parked on the north side of the grocery store parking lot early this morning. Whoever was driving it had backed it into the first space closest to the store," she said.

Sheriff Davis turned away from the phone and started barking orders for someone to check the empty parking space. "Okay, got my men on it. Anythin' else?"

"Not yet. I'm still working on it. MaryAnn Thompson saw the van before she entered the store. I'm thinking maybe this guy was watching and waiting for the perfect opportunity to kidnap someone." Brigid could almost see it in her mind's eye. The guy sitting there, hiding behind his newspaper, watching everyone enter the store and then leave. Did he know who he wanted to kidnap by the way they looked, or maybe it was something else altogether? "MaryAnn mentioned that he may have dark hair, but this guy was behind a newspaper, so she couldn't be sure."

"Okay, keep on it, Brigid. I know if there's anythin' to find, you'll find it."

"Thanks, Corey, I'll do my best," Brigid said before she ended the call. She was happy Sheriff Davis had so much confidence in her, because everything felt a little different this time.

CHAPTER EIGHT

Brigid left MaryAnn's home knowing she had one other person she needed to talk to before meeting Fiona and Missy at the bookstore. Eve Sterling. She'd heard that Eve had gone back to a day shift since her father-in-law had passed away, but Brigid wasn't sure what hours she worked. Crossing her fingers, she headed towards her house.

As she drove down the tree-lined street, Brigid took a deep breath and spent a moment enjoying the view. The trees were starting to get small leaves on them, so that the faintest bit of color was beginning to show. Pinks and greens were everywhere, making Brigid smile. As she pulled up to Eve's house, she saw a car in the driveway, hoping that meant Eve was at home. She parked next to it and turned off her engine.

"Brigid, is that you?" she heard a voice say as she got out of her car. Eve had stepped out onto the front porch, a flannel shirt wrapped tightly around her.

"Sure is, Eve. How are you doing?" Brigid said as she walked around her car and turned towards the front porch.

"Wonderful," Eve said smiling. "Why don't you come in and make yourself comfortable? What brings you here?"

Brigid stepped up onto the porch and sighed. "Nothing good, I'm afraid."

"Oh? Well then, we definitely need to sit down. Come on in."

Since she and her husband Frank were no longer having to care for his father in their home, they'd made some dramatic changes, and it looked so much better than the last time Brigid had been there. Previously the curtains had been drawn and everything was dusty and sad, as if all the life had been drained from their little home. Now, the place was spotless, and the curtains were wide open. The home had a much more inviting and pleasant feeling to it than it had before.

"Did you paint the inside of your house?" Brigid asked as she looked around while she sat down.

"Yes, I did," Eve said proudly. "I wanted something a bit more cheerful."

"I really like it," Brigid said admiringly. "It reminds me of a light mint chocolate chip ice cream."

"I know," Eve said as if it were a secret. "That's my favorite kind of ice cream, but don't tell anyone," she said with a laugh.

"Well, I should probably get right to it, Eve. I understand you had a conversation with Olivia Ford at the grocery store this morning. Is that correct?" Brigid asked.

Eve's eyebrows furrowed. "Yes. We're sort of friends. Why do you ask? What's happened?"

"It seems someone may have abducted Olivia from the parking lot of the grocery store. Security footage shows her leaving the store and heading to her car. She put her shopping bags in it, and then a white van pulled up beside her. Shortly after that, the van sped off and Olivia was gone. We're trying to figure out what happened." Brigid didn't enjoy having to be the bearer of bad news. This was the one real drawback to helping with criminal investigations.

"Oh, no," Eve gasped. She covered her mouth with her hand and her eyes teared up. "That's terrible. You mean, she never got to tell Mike?"

"Tell Mike what?" Brigid asked, confused.

"I'm not supposed to know anything. She swore me to secrecy,"

Eve whispered as if there were someone else in the room.

"Is it important to the case?"

Eve bit her lip. "I'm not sure. I only know about it because I was at the store the other day and ran into her. I wouldn't want to spoil it for her."

Brigid could see that Eve was clearly conflicted. She began picking at her fingernails as she bit her lip. Brigid could imagine how Eve felt. Knowing something that is someone else's secret, and then having them disappear had put Eve in a very delicate situation.

"Eve, why don't you tell me what it is? I promise I won't tell a soul. This way, if it is important to the case, at least someone on the inside knows about it," Brigid suggested. There was no way she would pass on the information if it wasn't relevant, but she was worried it could be something vital to help her find out where Olivia had gone.

"Alright," Eve said softly. "The other day when I ran into her, I noticed she was buying a pregnancy test kit. She thought she might be pregnant, but she wasn't sure. Olivia told me she was going to go home that night and take the test. When I ran into her this morning, I asked what the results were. She said they were positive, but she hadn't told her husband yet. She wanted to come up with a creative way to tell him."

Brigid felt the blood drain from her face. If Olivia was pregnant, that was all the more reason she needed to be safe. Who knew what her abductors could be doing to her? What if something had already happened? Time really was of the essence now. She was absolutely certain Olivia hadn't left of her own free will when she was making plans to tell her husband she was pregnant.

"In that case, it's even more important we find her as soon as possible. Can you remember anything odd about this morning? Possibly something having to do with a white van?"

Eve had been shaking her head no, but when Brigid mentioned the white van she stopped and looked at Brigid.

"Wait, there was a white van when I got there this morning," she said softly.

"What can you tell me about it?" Brigid said as she dug her notebook out of her purse.

"Well, there were two men standing outside of it. I think they may have been arguing, but I'm not sure. They were speaking quietly," she said.

"What makes you think they were arguing?" Brigid asked.

"Mostly from their body language," she said. "One was taller with dark hair and dark skin. I'm not sure of his ethnicity. The other man was lighter, kind of like me, but he also had black hair. The taller one was wearing a dark blue jacket and jeans while the younger, shorter one, had a white shirt and pants that kind of looked like sweat pants," Eve recalled. Her eyes looked off in the distance, as though she was seeing it all again in her mind.

"This is great information, Eve. Thanks," Brigid said as she wrote down everything Eve had told her.

"The thing is, I know I've seen that van somewhere before. It has damage to the front end, so I know it's the same one. I can't for the life of me remember where, though," she said, sounding frustrated.

"That's okay, even if you give me a few places it may have been, that will be a start. Do you think it was here in town?" Brigid asked.

"Yes, it was here in town. I think I saw it on the outskirts of town, maybe at a gas station or something, and it wasn't that long ago," she began. "I know I was on the main road that runs through Cottonwood Springs."

"You mean like out towards where the dress store is?" Brigid asked, surprised.

"Yes, in that direction. I heard the dress shop is having a going out of business sale," she said offhandedly.

"You saw the white van along that road somewhere?" Brigid repeated. "You're sure."

"Yes," Eve said confidently. "I'm not sure where it was, but it was along that road. Why?"

"I'm actually heading over there with my sister and Missy to see if they have anything I might be interested in buying for my wedding. I'll keep my eyes open when I go there," Brigid said.

"I heard you were getting married. Congratulations. I'm glad you're going to go out that way. Otherwise, now I'd feel like I had to go there. I'm certain that's where I saw it. Do you think those guys took Olivia?" she asked.

"I really don't know, Eve. Truthfully, they could have just been standing near the grocery store minding their own business. Who knows? But it would help to find the van first to make sure it's one and the same," Brigid commented. She stood up, tucking her notebook back in her purse. "I better go, so I can let Sheriff Davis know what you've told me. Believe me, you may have just helped immensely in solving this case."

"I sure hope so," Eve said as she walked Brigid to the door. "I hate to think that poor Olivia could be hurt. She's the nicest girl you could ever meet. You find her, you hear?"

"That's the plan. Again, thank you, Eve," Brigid said as she pulled open the door. "Keep her in your prayers."

"I will," Eve said as she shut the door.

This was the closest thing she'd had so far to a solid lead. As Brigid walked to her car, she looked around, scanning her surroundings. She was starting to feel paranoid, as if there was someone watching her. Her rational mind told her she was feeling that way because of what had happened to Olivia, but it was still a tough feeling to shake.

When she got back in her car, she started to pull out her phone to call Sheriff Corey Davis, but then she stopped. She knew he was incredibly busy, and so were all of his deputies. What if she called and told him that Eve was certain she'd seen the van on the road out of town, and then they couldn't find the van? It would be a huge waste of their time. She dropped her phone back in her purse. Plus, he'd told her he had to go out of town this afternoon.

I'll wait to call him until after I look for the van myself, she thought. *There's no point in calling Corey and distracting him or his deputies from what they're doing if it's not even there.*

Nodding to herself, she made her mind up. She'd be on the lookout for the van as they drove to the dress shop. If she saw it on the way there, she'd call him. If not, then no harm done, she wouldn't have wasted his time. She backed out of the driveway and headed toward her sister's bookstore. It was almost time to meet Fiona and Missy.

CHAPTER NINE

Brigid pulled up in front of the Read It Again bookstore right on time. As she walked through the front door, Fiona was already pulling on her jacket.

"Told you she'd be right on time," she said to Missy with a smirk.

"You know it," Brigid said proudly. "I can't stand to be late."

"I thought I'd drive, if that's okay with you?" Missy asked.

"Not a problem," Brigid said. "Just give me one minute, though." She turned to Holly, who was sitting behind the counter. "A woman has disappeared, and it looks like some other people may also have disappeared. I don't want you to go anywhere by yourself, okay?"

Holly nodded. "Sure," she said shrugging her shoulders.

Brigid patted the counter and smiled. "Thank you." Turning back to Fiona and Missy she said, "Okay, I'm ready. Let's go."

The three of them got into Missy's car, talking of wedding plans, dresses, and hairdos as they drove to the dress shop. They sounded as if they were high school girls again, getting ready for the prom. Brigid smiled as she sat in the back seat, listening to the conversation Fiona and Missy were having about strapless dresses. While she was enjoying the ride, she kept her eyes peeled for any sign of a white van, even though they weren't quite in the neighborhood Eve had described, but she didn't want to take any chances that she might miss it.

"So what kind of dress are you hoping to find?" Missy asked, as she looked at Brigid in the rearview mirror.

"I'm not sure. I'm thinking something that is fairly traditional, but with a little twist," she said, still scanning the area.

"That sounds fun. I think if I ever got married again, I'd do the same. I went the traditional route the first time. If I did it all over again, I definitely would do it with more flair," Missy said with a grin.

"I'd have a Halloween wedding," Fiona said as she chimed in.

"That's really weird," Missy said with a giggle.

"No, you wouldn't. That's not allowed," Brigid laughed. She sat up straighter as they approached the area Eve described.

"Hear me out," Fiona said. "With typical weddings, people are forced to dress up and all that jazz. With a Halloween one, they would still dress up, but in a costume. You could even have the ushers dress up as skeletons or zombies. It'd be fun."

"You're too much," Brigid said shaking her head.

"Hey, I bet you'd remember it," Fiona said.

"That's true. How could anyone forget something like that?" Missy asked.

Missy slowed down as they approached the small dress shop. It never really had a name, as the older woman who ran it had just converted part of her home into a store. Her shop was the place where kids would come to order prom dresses and tuxedos. Or at least they used to, before they could get everything they wanted from the internet.

Brigid sighed. She hadn't seen any vehicles that even resembled the white van. Feeling a little disappointed, she climbed out of the back of the car and walked towards the front of the dress shop.

There was a big handmade sign in the window that claimed everything was half price for the going-out-of-business sale. Brigid had to admit she loved a good sale, but it made her a bit sad to think the store would be closing.

Fiona held the door open for Missy and Brigid as they all stepped inside the small shop.

"Good afternoon, dears! My name is Dorothy, everything is half off. If you have something in mind, just let me know," the small older woman said as she greeted them. Her white hair was permed and combed out into what looked like a perfect white cotton ball. Her glasses almost seemed too heavy for her face and drooped down to the tip of her nose.

"I'm Fiona, this is my sister Brigid, and our friend, Missy. Brigid's getting married soon, so we thought we'd stop in and see what you have," Fiona said sweetly.

"Oh, a wedding. How lovely. Are you two going to be in it?" she asked, taking Fiona's hand.

"We sure are," she said.

"In that case, why don't you two head over there? You can look through the dresses that would be fitting for members of the wedding party. I'll take Brigid to the wedding dresses." She let go of Fiona and wrapped her bony hand around Brigid's arm. "This way, dear."

Missy and Fiona headed off to the area where Dorothy had pointed while she and Brigid walked into the next room.

"We built this room over twenty years ago," she said in her gentle, crackly voice. "Things used to be a lot different before people could jump on the computer and order whatever they want from it."

"This is a lovely room," Brigid said, as they stepped inside. There was lighting over each rack of dresses, making every sequin and bead sparkle and shimmer. There was also a seating area around a platform surrounded by mirrors on three sides. Brigid wondered how many brides had stood up on that platform, surrounded by their loved ones telling them how beautiful they looked. The carpeting was worn from all the feet that had sat on those chairs. Dorothy released Brigid's arm and sat down in a nearby chair.

"Wedding dresses are one of my favorite things to sell," Dorothy said. Brigid began to move along the rows, looking at the dresses. "Nobody's having a bad day when they go wedding dress shopping."

"What about those women who are 'bridezillas'?" Brigid asked.

"Oh now, they just know what they want is all. Nothing wrong with that," Dorothy said.

Brigid looked at the older woman and smiled. Her calm manner had a soothing effect on Brigid. It was as though she was a sanctuary in an otherwise blustery world.

Spying a dress with a bit of color in it, Brigid's pulled it out and held it up in front of her. It was all lace and off the shoulder. From the bottom up, embroidered roses embellished the tulle that covered the skirt.

"Now that's a dress," Dorothy said. "Not for just any bride."

"It is pretty," Brigid admitted. "Let me think about it."

"Sure, sure. Look around first. I'll go see how the other two are doing. If you want to try something on, the dressing room's right over there." She pointed to a door in the far corner.

"Thank you," Brigid said kindly.

After Dorothy left, she continued to look at the dresses. There were all kinds of styles. Empire waists, fitted, and some that looked like they should be worn by a princess. They were all extremely beautiful, but none of them spoke to her quite like the first one she'd seen. Eventually, she decided to try it on. It had looked to be about her size.

Once inside the dressing room, Brigid quickly slipped off her clothing and stepped into the dress. She couldn't zip it all the way up by herself, but she came close. Trying to see what she looked like in the narrow mirror in the dressing room wasn't allowing her to get the broad view she wanted, so she decided to step out into the main room where the wider mirrors were located to get a better view.

She walked out of the room, lifting the skirt so she wouldn't accidentally step on it.

"Oh!" she heard as she looked up. Fiona, Missy, and Dorothy were standing there, apparently waiting to show her a couple of dresses.

"Brigid, you look beautiful," Missy said.

Brigid felt embarrassed as she felt the blood rush to her face. "Thank you," she said quietly.

"I love it," Fiona said.

Dorothy rushed over and made quick work of the zipper, her hands suddenly feeling much more capable and stronger than they'd been when she'd gripped Brigid's arm.

"Come on, let's get you on the platform in front of the mirrors. Follow me ladies." She walked over to the seating area and gestured for Brigid to step up on it. Once in front of the mirrors, Brigid had to admit the dress looked absolutely gorgeous. It was perfect for her figure, hugging her hips, and flattering her subtle curves.

"It needs to be taken in here," Dorothy said as she began to move around Brigid. She lifted and tugged at the fabric, pulling pins from what seemed like thin air. Once she was done pinning, she laid out the skirt before stepping back. "Stunning. What do you think?"

Brigid wasn't sure what magic Dorothy had managed to do with her pins, but the dress looked even better than it had a few minutes earlier. If Brigid blocked off her face, she wouldn't have believed that was her body wearing such a remarkable dress.

"I love it," she admitted.

"I made this one myself," Dorothy said as she ran her finger along the short sleeve.

"Did you really?" Brigid asked, shocked.

"I sure did, back before my eyes got too bad to see what I was sewing," she admitted. "It's been here a while now, just waiting for the right bride-to-be to come along."

"Awww," Missy said getting a bit teary-eyed. That's so sweet."

"I think you should get it," Fiona said. "It's one of a kind, and it looks like it was made for you. I swear, I don't think you could ever find anything better."

Brigid turned to the side, admiring the dress a little longer. She tried to imagine what Holly and Linc would say when they saw it.

"I'll take it," Brigid found herself saying.

"Wonderful," Dorothy said as she clapped her hands. "Your friends have a couple of dresses they want your opinion on, but first, we'll get you out of that dress. I'll make the alterations and have it ready for you in a couple weeks. I'll get your number, and call you when it's ready."

After changing out of the dress, it was Missy and Fiona's turn to try on dresses. Eventually, Fiona told them that she would buy whatever style dress Brigid and Missy liked the best. Brigid told them their dresses didn't have to match, as long as the colors were spring-like, that was all that mattered. She was on cloud nine. Not only had she figured out the location of the wedding, but now she also had a dress. The plans were definitely moving forward.

CHAPTER TEN

For the next forty-five minutes, they tried on dress after dress. Fiona was a bit more decisive, like her sister, but she and Missy still couldn't pass up the opportunity to try on the various dresses. Finally, Missy settled on a soft teal chiffon dress with a high waist. Fiona decided she really liked a lavender dress that was fitted with sequins.

"I think I really love the bling," Fiona said as she admired the dress in the mirror. Once they'd decided, Dorothy began to tuck and pin each of them in their dresses. When she was finished, the dresses fit them perfectly.

"I'm going to send you an invitation to the wedding," Brigid promised Dorothy.

"Oh, you don't have to do that," she said waving her away.

"No, I insist. I would love to have you there. You should be able to see your dresses in action," Brigid said.

Dorothy smiled. "Thank you. That would be wonderful."

She led them to her cash register and rang up the three dresses. The total before the sale would have been a good price for the custom-fitted outfits, but once the sale price was deducted, Brigid was ecstatic. She handed Dorothy the money and thanked her for being so helpful.

"It's my pleasure, honey," she said. "It's all I've done for so long, I wouldn't know what else to do."

"So why close?" Missy asked.

"Well, my health isn't quite what it used to be. I'm getting around okay today, but some days aren't so good. All our children are grown and have moved away. It just seems like the right time to let it go. Now I have to get rid of all these dresses." Although Dorothy smiled when she said it, Brigid was sure she could sense a hint of sadness.

"I suppose that's true," Fiona said softly. "I can't imagine the day I would have to close the doors to my store."

Dorothy stepped out from behind the counter and began to ask Fiona about her store. Brigid still felt as though the woman was greatly underpricing her dresses. She would have gotten three times as much for them if she'd been in a better location with more customers. Quickly, while Dorothy was distracted, Brigid pulled a couple of hundred-dollar bills from her wallet.

Finding a slip of paper and a pen, she hurriedly wrote, "Treat yourself" before sliding the money and the note just underneath the corner of a catalog on the counter. When Dorothy eventually got back to the counter, she couldn't miss it. Brigid felt much better about herself as she joined her sister and her friend.

"We should probably get going before the guys wonder what we're up to," she said.

"It was nice meeting you girls," Dorothy called out as they left the store. "Stop by anytime, and tell your friends."

"What a nice woman," Missy said as they returned to her car.

"Those prices were something else," Fiona said. "If she wasn't trying to close down her business, those prices would."

"I left a little extra for her," Brigid admitted.

"Did you really?" Missy asked as they climbed in the car.

"Yeah. I wouldn't have been able to live with myself, otherwise," Brigid admitted.

"You have a good heart, Brigid Barnes," Missy said. "Made from solid gold. Not many people would do that."

"She always has been a good person. Always trying to do what's right," Fiona said, smiling back at her sister.

Brigid had returned to the back seat again, planning on watching for the white van she'd been looking for earlier. Truthfully, she didn't expect to find it, but she couldn't just not look. Until it was located, she'd probably spend most of her time out in public trying to find it.

Pulling out onto the road, Missy and Fiona started chatting again, leaving Brigid to herself, which was fine, because she needed time to think. If these people were from out of town, they had to have somewhere they were staying. She doubted they were sleeping in the van as it was still quite cold at night even though spring was starting to break winter's firm grip. She was busy mentally creating a list of places in town to check when she spotted something white parked not far off the road.

Shaking herself, she realized what she'd seen was a white van. It was parked on the back side of the old Star Motel. Not many people stayed at the old seedy motel unless they were broke or didn't know any better.

"Hey, Missy? Would you pull in here?" Brigid asked as she pointed to the gas station located next to the motel.

"Sure, do you need to use the ladies' room?" Missy asked, but Brigid didn't answer. Instead, she patiently waited until the car came to a stop, and then she hurriedly got out.

"What is she doing?" Missy asked when she realized Brigid wasn't going to the gas station.

"I don't have a clue," Fiona said, as they watched her.

Brigid half-walked, half-jogged across the empty parking lot in the direction of the van. It was parked in the very last parking space behind the motel, which sat angled on the property. From the looks of it, the van may have been sitting there when they first drove by, but coming from the other direction, it had been hidden from view.

Reaching for her phone, she realized she'd left her purse in the car. *No matter,* she thought. *I'll just get closer to it so I can make sure it's the same van, then I'll head back to the car.* Drawing closer, Brigid held her breath, as the front of the van came into view. There it was, the damage both Eve and MaryAnn had both described. Part of her told her she should turn around and head back to the car. She knew where the drivers of the van were staying, at least for now, and she also knew the sensible thing for her to do was return to the car and call the sheriff.

Her body didn't listen to her mind, and her feet continued to carry her closer to the van. No matter what she rationally thought, she knew she wasn't done yet. She couldn't quite get her feet to turn around just yet. Once she was beside the van, she walked around to the back, looking for the license plate.

"New Mexico, XJB 102," she whispered to herself. She continued to recite it, as her feet carried her to the motel room the vehicle was parked in front of. Steeling her nerve, she knocked on the door.

Brigid heard the television volume turned up loudly to a news channel. She knocked again, louder this time.

Suddenly the door jerked open, and a young man with black hair was standing in the doorway. His white shirt was wrinkled, and he was wearing sweat pants. He fit the description Eve had given her of the younger man.

"Oh, excuse me. I thought this was my friend's room," she lied.

He gave her a lecherous grin. "We could be friends, *chica,"* he said giving her a wink.

"Sorry," she said, waving as an older man joined him at the door. A chill ran through Brigid's body when she realized he fit Eve's description, too. Hurrying away, she didn't slow down until she heard the door click behind her. She turned to make sure they weren't following her before letting out a huge breath of air.

"What in the devil was that all about?" Fiona asked as she climbed back in the car.

"That's the van," Brigid said, winded. Her heart was beating so fast she thought it was going to explode. "And the two guys in the motel room match the description Eve and MaryAnn gave me."

"So you decided to go say 'what's up' to them?" her sister shrieked.

"Pretty much," Brigid said as she clicked her seatbelt.

Missy pulled back out onto the road. "If I'd known you were having me pull over so you could try to do some of your vigilante stuff, I would have kept on driving," she said disapprovingly. "What would you have done if they snatched you right then and there?"

"I knew you two were watching me. If anything bad happened, you could have called Corey," she pointed out.

"Yeah, and hope you weren't diced up or put on the black market in the meantime!" Fiona yelled.

"I'm sorry," Brigid said. "I wasn't really thinking. I just know we have to find these guys fast, and I didn't want to wait. Now, we have the license number on their van, and we know where they're staying."

Missy and Fiona looked at each other. "True," Missy said.

"Shouldn't I pull over so you can call Sheriff Davis and tell him what you've found?" Missy asked.

"No, he's out-of-town this afternoon attending some meeting with other nearby county sheriffs and won't be back in town until later today. I'll call him as soon as he gets back," Brigid replied.

"All we have to do is tell Sheriff Davis, so he can arrest them," Brigid pointed out. She couldn't help but feel as if she'd accomplished something today. First a wedding dress, then, finding two bad guys. It was turning out to be a very good day.

CHAPTER ELEVEN

Holly was watching the clock, counting down the time before she could close up Fiona's bookstore. There were two ladies who had been wandering around in the store for quite a while looking at books, which helped pass the time. Holly loved to watch people as they selected their books and moved through the store. There was something about watching people when they didn't realize they were being watched. It was as if you could see who they really were by their mannerisms. It simply fascinated Holly.

She'd recently been debating what kind of a career she wanted after she finished college. Part of her had been leaning toward police work, but once she'd started working at the bookstore, she began broadening her horizons. Perhaps her love for watching people meant she should explore psychology or something like that? Holly knew she was getting to that point in her life when she needed to make a choice, but she still felt very uncertain about the future.

"Are you finished looking?" she heard the shorter brunette woman ask the blonde.

"I think so," she replied.

"Are you ready to check out?" Holly asked as the two women approached the counter.

"Yes, but it's just so hard to choose. There are so many good books here," the first woman said.

"I know what you mean," Holly said smiling. "That's why I like working here. There are a lot more perks than just the coffee."

"I bet," the other one said. "I don't think I'd ever see a paycheck if I worked in a bookstore."

"It's definitely a challenge," Holly admitted. "At least I don't have to worry about bills or anything yet."

She handed the first woman her bag with the books she'd purchased and her receipt and started scanning the second woman's books.

"That must be nice. I wish I would have thought to work at a bookstore when I was a teenager," the brunette said.

"Agreed!" exclaimed the blonde. "Or even the library."

"Oh, yeah, the library. That would have been the best."

Holly wished them both a good evening and followed them to the door. They began talking about the jobs they had when they were teenagers and started to compare whose was the worst. The brunette said she'd been a waitress while the other one had worked on her grandfather's farm.

As far as Holly was concerned, neither job sounded like much fun. She threw the deadbolt on the front door and turned off the open sign. She was five minutes early, but she didn't think there was going to be a rush on the store this close to closing time. Most people were out enjoying the spring weather.

Holly stood in the window and watched the trees sway in the gentle evening breeze. People were hurrying home from work or wherever they'd been. Soon they'd be sitting down to dinner and watching the evening news.

Brigid's words echoed in her ear. "A woman has disappeared. I don't want you to go anywhere by yourself, okay?"

"But I've been going places by myself my whole life," Holly said aloud to herself. "Nothing's ever happened to me." Holly tried to take the warning seriously, but people went missing all the time. That didn't mean someone kidnapped them. Most of them probably disappeared on purpose.

Holly recalled all the times her mom had gone out on a bender and not come home for days. The first few times Holly had been worried. Of course, she'd only been around seven years old or so back then. It didn't take long before Holly had learned how to take care of herself.

Her phone buzzed with a text, and she picked it up to check it. It was her aunt asking how long Holly wanted to stay with her and what dates she had in mind. She wanted to take Holly to their favorite places while she visited.

Holly smiled. She had to admit she was really looking forward to this trip. Although she'd never been out of Colorado, she'd always been curious about what the rest of the United States was like. When her mother died, she hadn't wanted to move out of state and away from everything she'd ever known, but going to visit her aunt was a whole different thing.

Ever since she'd found out she lived in Springfield, Missouri, Holly had been on the internet looking at images and checking the place out. Although it wasn't a large city like Denver, it was still bigger than the Cottonwood Springs Holly was used to. She'd never been to Denver before she'd started living with Brigid, so bigger cities were somewhat new to her. She tried to imagine what life would have been like if she hadn't asked Brigid if she could live with her. Would she have loved it in the city or would she feel out of place?

Shaking off the thought, she decided it didn't matter. After all, this was her home now and Brigid was her sorta' mom. Sometimes she wondered if Brigid regretted letting her stay, especially now that she was going to be marrying Linc. Holly loved them both, and they were great people, but that didn't mean they wanted a teenage girl hanging around. What if they decided to adopt kids? Brigid was a little too old to have her own, but since neither one of them had had children with their previous spouses, maybe now they'd want to.

Women were having babies later in life, so it wasn't out of the question for them to adopt one. Brigid didn't think they'd have any problem being accepted. Brigid seemed fairly healthy, and Linc acted as though he was much younger. If it weren't for the grey hair and wrinkles, she'd have been fooled.

Holly scanned the rows of books in the bookstore, looking for any that needed to be put back before sitting back down at the register. Closing the bookstore for Fiona wasn't hard. All Holly had to do was straighten it up, count the money in the register, and put the cash drawer in the safe. Easy.

After counting the money and putting it away, she looked over at the box of new books in the back room. Normally, she'd just head home, but she was dragging her feet tonight. She didn't want to bother Linc, and she was sure she would have heard from Brigid if they were finished shopping. While she looked through the new books, she debated whether or not she should call them.

She pulled out a book that looked interesting and tucked it in her backpack. Fiona had told her numerous times she could borrow a book to read if she was gentle with it. She could probably read this one in a day or so. It was about a young girl solving a mystery surrounding her family. Holly felt like she could identify with that.

Sighing, she decided against calling anyone to pick her up. What was one more ride home going to hurt? One of Holly's favorite parts of her day was when she was able to ride her bike in the spring air. Winter had been brutal, and she hadn't ridden as much as she would have liked. Now though, she could. Why pass up great riding weather?

Pulling on her backpack, she pushed her bike out into the alley. She flipped off the lights before locking the door behind her. Stomach growling, she pulled out her wallet.

"Just enough money for a bite to eat," she said. She wasn't sure what Brigid had planned for dinner, but she was starving. She could swing by somewhere on the way home and get something quick.

Holly climbed on her bike and began pedaling. Rather than heading home, she circled around to make a quick trip by the burger place. If she hurried, nobody would be any the wiser she hadn't called for a ride. She began to pedal faster, hoping to make good time.

CHAPTER TWELVE

"I'm so glad we were all able to find dresses at such a great price," Missy gushed as they pulled up to the bookstore.

"Me, too," sighed Brigid. "Now I can mark another thing off my list."

"Let me talk to a lady in the congregation about the wedding cake. I've heard she does spectacular work," Missy suggested.

"Oh, is it Lewellen?" Fiona asked as they sat in the car with the engine running.

"Yes, it is," Missy said, nodding.

"I've seen her work and I agree. She does a great job," Fiona said turning to her sister. "I'm sure she could come up with something you'd love."

"Thanks. I'd appreciate it if you'd talk to her," Brigid said. She looked at the darkened store front and sighed, "Looks like we missed Holly."

"That makes things easier for me," Fiona said. "Now I don't have to be the one to close up the store."

"I just hope she called Linc, since I told her not to go anywhere alone until those kidnappers are caught," Brigid said as she picked up her purse.

"I'm sure she did," Missy said brightly. "Holly's probably at home now, anxious to hear how the dress shopping excursion went."

"I hope so," Brigid said as she scooted toward the door. "I won't be able to sleep well until these people are caught."

"I don't think anyone will," Fiona said in agreement. They told each other goodbye and then went their separate ways.

As Brigid drove home, she kept an eye on the sides of the road just in case Holly had decided to go home alone. She knew the route Holly took to and from the bookstore, so when she pulled up to her house and didn't see Holly's bike on the porch, her brow furrowed.

"Maybe she's over at Linc's," she said aloud to herself, since the lights in her house were all dark, she could tell no one was home. After she'd unlocked the front door and gone inside, she pulled out her phone and called Linc.

"Well, hello, beautiful," he said as he answered her call.

"Did you pick Holly up from the bookstore?" she asked.

"No, why? Was I supposed to?" he asked.

"Well, not really. I told her that since Olivia was missing, I didn't want her to ride around on her bike and go places alone. She was supposed to call me or you to get a ride home rather than ride her bike. I followed her route home and didn't see her. I assumed she was with you." Brigid felt a knot beginning to form in her stomach.

"She's not here at my house. Why don't you see if she's at a friend's house? Maybe she stopped there for something. I'll be over in just a minute," Linc said as he ended the call.

Brigid went to her text messages and typed up a message. She copied it and pasted it, sending it to Holly's boyfriend's father and her other friends' parents. She crossed her fingers as she sent each one, hoping that someone would text her back that she was with them.

While she waited to hear from them, Brigid opened the back door and let Jett come inside. He trotted in and headed down the hall towards Holly's room before returning to the great room where he let out a small whine.

"Yeah, I know Jett. She's not here," Brigid said as she tried her best to stay calm. Her phone vibrated, and she checked the message. As she was reading the first one saying Holly wasn't there, the rest began to come through, all stating they hadn't seen her.

Brigid stood up and began to pace. Where could Holly be? Torn between looking for Holly and calling Sheriff Davis about the possible kidnappers, she couldn't decide what to do first. Jett, upset at not finding Holly in her room, flopped down on the loveseat in the corner that served as his bed.

"I know, I'm worried, too, big guy," Brigid said to Jett as she sat down on the couch. She couldn't bring herself to sit back, so she simply perched on the edge of the cushion, ready to spring into action.

A knock on the door pulled Brigid away from thoughts of Holly being kidnapped. "Come in," she called out, knowing who it was from the knock.

"Have you found her yet?" Linc asked as he stepped through the door and shut it behind him. Jett hopped up from his spot and slowly went over to Linc. He seemed to sense that something was wrong.

"No. I messaged Wade's dad, along with all the other friends' parents she's been to visit. Nobody's seen or heard from her for a while." Brigid stood up and began to pace again. "Linc, what if they took her?"

"You don't know for sure if Olivia's been taken," Linc began, but Brigid silenced him with a shake of her head.

"I saw them, Linc. When I talked to Eve Sterling, she told me about two men who were driving the vehicle that appears to have been used to take her. She described the van to me, and I saw it when Missy, Fiona and I went dress shopping. I made Missy pull over at a gas station near the motel where it was parked. I went to their room and…," she was interrupted by Linc.

"You did what?" Linc bellowed. The sheer volume of Linc's voice shocked Brigid.

"The van was right there. I had to make sure it was the same men that Eve and MaryAnn had seen. I didn't want to send the sheriff over there on a fool's errand," Brigid said trying to defend herself.

"Of all the reckless things," Linc muttered as he stood up. He walked over to Brigid and pulled her into his arms. He held her for a long time before finally letting her go. "Brigid, please listen to me. You have to think about the possible consequences of what you're doing. You can't go off halfcocked."

"I knew what I was doing," Brigid said, jutting her chin out. "Missy and Fiona could see me the entire time. And don't worry, they've already yelled at me about it."

"Good, someone's got to talk some sense into you," he muttered as he shook his head. "I always knew you were brave, but that was a crazy thing to do."

"Linc, I'm worried they may have taken Holly," she said as she redirected them back to the subject at hand.

"Let's go drive around and look for her. Leave a note for her to call us, just in case we miss her, and she shows up here," he said.

Brigid nodded and found a piece of paper. She quickly scrawled out a note directing Holly to stay put and to call her as soon as she read the note. After writing it, Brigid took a deep breath to calm herself. She could feel her hands shaking as her mind began to jump to conclusions. Gripping the edge of the counter, Brigid leaned over the paper, silently hoping nothing bad had happened to Holly.

"Relax," Linc said as he began to rub her shoulders. "I'm sure she's fine. Not everything has to end in tragedy. She's probably on her way home right now. I bet she just took a different way home or something. Try not to worry for now."

"I know. I shouldn't automatically assume the worst. It's just that I'm so worried, and now this, along with everything else," she let her sentence trail off.

"I agree," Linc said, turning towards her and once again pulling her into his arms. A few unbidden tears streamed down Brigid's cheeks as she allowed herself to sink into Linc's embrace for just a few moments, letting everything around them disappear while she caught her breath. Once he was sure she was calm, he released her. "You ready?"

She nodded and picked up her purse. "Come on, Jett," she called. Together they left the house, and she shut the door behind them.

"Brigid, we'll drive up and down every street if we have to," Linc promised. "We'll find her, I promise."

As they were walking to his truck, Brigid caught sight of a familiar flashing light on a bicycle. "Holly?" she called out.

"Yeah?" a familiar voice replied.

"Oh, thank goodness," Brigid gasped, as the young girl came into view. She fell against the truck in relief. Jett ran towards Holly, barking and wagging his tail.

"What's wrong?" Holly asked, as she got off her bike and walked it up the driveway.

"We've been worried about you," Linc said in a serious tone.

"Why? I was fine," Holly said, completely oblivious to Linc and Brigid's concern.

"I told you to get a ride home," Brigid began. "I told you there are people who have disappeared." Brigid tried to remain calm, but she couldn't. After everything that had happened, and then being worried about Holly, she started to cry again.

"I'm sorry," Holly said softly. "I didn't want to bother anyone, and I thought I'd be home before anyone knew any different."

"Well, I knew, and I've been worried out of my mind," Brigid said as she rushed over to the young girl. She pulled Holly into a tight hug, squeezing her so tight it was hard for her to breathe.

"I… can't… breathe," Holly gasped.

"Holly, you really scared us," Linc said, disappointment clearly showing on his face.

"I'm sorry, I didn't mean to scare you," Holly said, her eyes wide.

"I'm just glad you're okay. Next time, when Brigid tells you to get a ride, just call. You won't be bothering me," he said.

Holly nodded as Brigid released her. "It won't happen again. I promise," she said.

"Let's all go in the house," Brigid said as she regained her composure. "I still need to call Sheriff Davis."

CHAPTER THIRTEEN

"Hi Corey, it's Brigid," she said after Sheriff Davis answered his cell phone. "I have more information for you."

"Great. I just got back to Cottonwood Springs from a meetin' with some sheriffs from other nearby counties where we was comparin' notes 'bout all the people that gone missin' 'round here. I fer sure wanna' talk to ya' if'n ya' gots some info fer me. But listen, I'm not too far from your place. I'll jes' swing by, and ya' can tell me in person, okay?" he asked.

"Not a problem, Corey. I'll be here," she said.

"See ya' in a few," he said.

"So, tell me," Linc began. "What have you been up to all day? Last I knew you were going to be doing wedding stuff, and now you're in the middle of another investigation."

Brigid thought back to this morning and could hardly believe everything that had happened. She woke up in the morning with the intention of talking to a florist about flowers for her wedding and getting some editorial work done. Instead, she'd ended up roped into a missing persons case and dress shopping. That didn't even take into account coming face to face with the potential suspects and being scared half to death that Holly had been taken as well.

After giving Linc a play by play of her day, he let out a low whistle.

"I don't know how you do it. The situation with Holly was the first time I've ever seen you lose your cool and even that wasn't too terrible. You are amazing," he marveled.

"I don't know about all that," Brigid said as she brushed away his compliment.

"It's true. Things just roll off you like water off a duck's back. Nothing gets to you. I'm envious. I was stuck behind my computer looking at numbers all day," Linc grumbled.

The sound of a car door closing made Jett raise his head from where he'd been laying at both of their feet.

"Sounds like Sheriff Davis is here," Brigid said as she stood up and walked over to the door. She pulled it open as he was raising his hand to knock on the door.

"Hi, Brigid," he said as he touched the tip of his hat with his hand before pulling it off while he stepped inside. "Linc."

"Hello, Sheriff," Linc said.

Sheriff Davis turned to Brigid, "So what ya' got fer me?"

"Come sit down and I'll explain," she said. Once she'd offered him something to drink, and they'd all gotten settled, she began to tell him what she'd found out.

"I took notes on what MaryAnn and Eve saw which you can read later. Anyway, there are two men who drive the white van. They're staying at the Star Motel, that seedy motel just outside of town. When Missy, Fiona, and I went dress shopping, I saw the white van parked there. Missy pulled into the gas station next to the motel. I went to the room the van was parked in front of and knocked on the door," Brigid began.

"What were ya' thinking? Ya' do realize ya' don't have a badge, right?" Sheriff Davis asked, horrified.

"I'm aware of that. I just wanted to see if it was the same men that Eve says she saw standing outside the van, and I'm certain they're the same guys. Time is of the essence, Corey. I think you should go out to the motel and arrest them. We've got to get Olivia back as soon as possible," Brigid insisted.

"I agree with ya' about Olivia, but I can't jes' arrest them with no probable cause, ya' know that," Sheriff Davis said as he shook his head.

"You don't understand, Corey. There's something special about Olivia that you don't know about," Brigid said. "No one is supposed to know anything about it yet." Brigid didn't want to tell them Olivia's secret, but at the same time she felt the sheriff might feel differently if he knew.

"What are ya' talkin' about?" he asked, confused.

"Look, she wasn't telling people yet, so this has to stay quiet. She hadn't even told Mike. Just because she's gone missing doesn't mean her private affairs need to be spread all over town," Brigid began.

Sheriff Davis nodded. "Okay, I'll keep it under wraps long as I can. What's the big secret?"

Brigid bit her lip before saying, "She's pregnant."

Both men were silent for a few moments as they processed what she'd just told them. Linc was the first to speak, "Well, that's not good."

"No, no it ain't," Sheriff Davis said thoughtfully. "Poor Mike."

"Now you see why I want you to bring them in?" Brigid asked.

"Brigid, I understand what yer' sayin'," he began, "but ya' need to understand somethin'. These guys ain't necessarily gonna' start singin' jes' because I slap some cuffs on 'em. Most likely, they got somewhere they're keepin' her 'til someone else comes to take her away. If we bring 'em in, and we can't get 'em to talk, she may wind up bein' permanently gone and lost in the wind. We'll never find her then." He began chewing on his lip while his eyes drifted off into the distance.

"Well, in that case, what do you suggest?" Brigid asked. She saw his point, but that didn't make it any easier to accept. Just the thought of a young woman taken against her will was sickening. The fact that she was pregnant added another layer of concern to an already horrible situation.

"First we need to watch 'em," he said as he continued to think. "Need to see where they go." He lifted his eyes to Brigid. "Did'ja happen to get a license number on that white van?"

She nodded and dug out her notebook from her purse. She flipped to the page and showed it to the sheriff. Turning to the radio on his shoulder, he pushed a button. "101 to 107," he said into it and then waited.

"101 this is 107," came a response.

"107, I need ya' to see if you can locate that vehicle we was lookin' fer earlier. I'm gonna' text you the plate number and probable location," he said as he pulled out his phone.

"10-4, do you need me to speak with them?" came the response.

"Negative," Sheriff Davis said. "Fer now I want ya' to jes' observe. I'll take over after a while."

"10-4, will do."

Sheriff Davis finished typing on his phone before looking back up at them. "Didn't want to say too much over the radio and tip 'em off. Some of them people have police radio scanners, and I don't want 'em knowin' we're watchin' 'em."

"Good thinking," Linc said in agreement. "You just never know who's listening."

"Exactly. We need the element of surprise on our side with this one. Like I told ya' earlier, I've been talkin' with the sheriffs from our neighborin' counties today. A few of 'em have some people who've gone missin' recently. Some say they ain't sure if they're runaways or what since there weren't any witnesses that they know of.

"Close by there's a missin' boy of around thirteen and a twenty-year-old woman. The boy may jes' be a runaway. The woman's car was found broken-down on the side of the highway, but there weren't no sign of her." Sheriff Davis shook his head. "For their sakes, I hope they aren't wrapped up in all of this."

"I agree," Brigid said, "but at the same time I do. That way if we find Olivia, we'll find those missing persons too."

"Not if, Brigid, when," Sheriff Davis said. "Don't lose hope now."

"I'm sorry, you're right. When we find them."

"I better go so I can watch the van myself. Ain't that I don't trust my deputies, but if she's pregnant, I sure don't want there bein' any accidents. I also don't wanna' have to share that info with the entire department," he said as he stood up.

"Wait," Brigid said as she stood up too. "Corey, I want to go with you."

"Don't know if that's wise," Sheriff Davis began.

"Look, I've seen these guys. I've seen the van. You won't know for sure if it's the same guys if you don't let me go," she explained.

The sheriff paused, looking at Brigid and trying to decide if it was a wise choice or not.

"You know she's going to do what she wants. You might as well let her go with you," Linc said. "She's a stubborn one." He smirked at the last part, almost as if he was proud of her when she was stubborn.

"Don't need to tell me that. Well aware of it," Sheriff Davis said. He debated for a moment longer before finally relenting. "Okay, but bring a jacket with ya'. Likely to get purty cold while we jes' sit."

Brigid rushed to the hall closet and tugged a jacket off of a coat hanger. "Linc, will you…," she began, but he held up his hand.

"Say no more. I'll hang out here until you get back," he said with a smile.

She rushed over and gave him a kiss. "Thank you."

"Ya' ready?" Sheriff Davis asked.

"Definitely," Brigid answered.

CHAPTER FOURTEEN

The sun had almost left the sky and it was getting darker by the minute. The landscape flew by as they headed towards their destination. While Brigid rode in the unmarked sheriff's car driven by Sheriff Davis, she let her mind wander to her wedding plans and to the couple of places that she and Linc had narrowed down to go for their honeymoon.

They were still fairly much up in the air about it, but each one was a location where she'd always wanted to go. She knew it sounded kind of crazy, but she'd written a report on the Alamo when she'd been in high school, and San Antonio was definitely one of the places on her list. To say she was excited was an understatement.

"So how long ago did ya' see the van over at the Star Motel?" Sheriff Davis asked, pulling her out of her momentary reverie and back to the present.

"I'm not sure. It's probably been about two or three hours," she admitted. It felt like forever, but it could have been even less. She mentally kicked herself for not checking the time when she'd been there.

He nodded as he drove through town and headed towards the Star Motel. "That's not too terrible long," he stated. "Hopefully my deputy was able to get eyes on the suspect vehicle and make sure they didn't go nowhere yet."

"They didn't look like they were planning on going anywhere when they opened the door," Brigid recalled. As she brought the men to mind, she felt anger begin to course through her veins. To think they were taking innocent people away from their families and for what?

"That's good. Ya' don't mind if I grab a quick bite, do ya'? Ain't had nothin' to eat since breakfast." He turned to look at her and she shook her head.

"Please do," she said. "You won't bother me."

"You want anythin'?" he asked as he turned off the road and pulled into the drive-thru lane of a local fast food place.

"No, thank you," Brigid said. "I'm good."

"Suit yourself," he said as he rolled down his window and began to order. He ordered a patty melt, fries, and a Coke. When he added an extra order of fries and Coke, Brigid crossed her arms and gave him a look.

Giving her an innocent grin, he chuckled. "What's that look fer?"

"You didn't have to do that, you know," she said.

"I know. Don't worry, I get a discount anyway. If ya' really don't want 'em, we'll feed 'em to the birds or somethin'. By the way, the fries are baked, not deep fat-fried, and their patty melts are the best. I always order the baked fries, jes' so I can justify the rest of it."

In a matter of minutes, they had their food and were back out on the road. Corey turned towards the outskirts of town, and Brigid couldn't help but sigh.

"What's up?" Corey asked.

"I just don't understand why anyone would take another human being. What's the point of it all?" She'd been thinking about how worried she'd been that Holly had been taken, and she couldn't imagine the things that were probably going through Mike Ford's mind at this point.

"For a lotta' reasons, from what I hear. Recently it seems human traffickin' has become a very lucrative business to criminals," he began.

"Why here?" Brigid asked. "I can understand that happening in some of the bigger cities, but why come to a small town? Because we're easy targets?" She was feeling put out with the whole world at that moment and needed some sort of explanation. What was happening to Olivia? Was she being treated well enough that her baby was still safe, or was it too late? It was all pretty overwhelming and was beginning to make her head swim.

"Well, kinda'," he said. "Theory is that people in the city are a bit more cautious these days. Ya' know how it is when ya' go there. Everyone's worried about themselves, and ya' can't even accidentally bump into someone in the store and say 'excuse me' without getting glared at or worse."

Brigid nodded. She'd seen some of the same things.

"These smaller towns, though?" Corey continued, "Folks are friendlier, even to people they don't know. People leave their doors unlocked, trust people enough to walk up to their vehicles without payin' much attention to their surroundins'. Think the bad guys have jes' learned it's fairly easy to grab someone when they're more trustin'."

Brigid shook her head. "I don't know if that's a good or bad thing."

"I'd say it's both," he observed. "Where'd ya' say they was parked at the motel?"

"On the back side," she said. "Kind of on the end. You can see their van when you're coming from the north."

Corey turned into a parking lot across the street from the gas station where Brigid had asked Missy to pull into earlier that day. The business that had originally been there had long ago closed, leaving a shell of a building with a faded 'for sale' sign in the window.

"I don't see the van," Brigid said softly.

"Don't worry. They'll come back," he said confidently.

As he pulled out a couple of French fries from his fast food bag, Corey took out his phone and began to punch in some numbers.

"Hey, Pete. Where are ya'?" He listened quietly for a few minutes, occasionally tossing a French fry in his mouth.

"Yeah, I'm sittin' in the unmarked over in the old Johnson's parking lot. Ya' can head on home now. I'll let ya' know if I need ya' for anythin'. Keep yer' phone handy." He put his phone back in his pocket and turned his attention to his patty melt.

"Have you spoken to Olivia's husband, Mike?" Brigid asked.

"Yeah," Sheriff Davis said around bites of his patty melt. "I let him know earlier we had a few leads we were pursuin' and that I'd let him know in the mornin' how those turned out. Doubt if he's gonna' get much sleep tonight, though."

"So you didn't really tell him anything," Brigid surmised.

"No," he said chuckling. "Not that I didn't want to, but I've learned that sometimes it's best to give 'em less information in the beginnin'. Otherwise, people tend to do their own investigation and sometimes that can really mess everythin' up. Course it was a little harder in this case, him bein' my best friend and all."

Brigid gave him a pointed look. "Are you trying to say something here?" she teased.

"Yer' different. I know ya' got a good head on your shoulders, although ya' do have a habit of going off halfcocked, but ya' still cover yerself' when ya' do. Like this afternoon. Ya' knew ya' had people watchin' your back in case somethin' were to happen. Not everyone's that smart or quick witted. Ya' saw an opportunity, and ya' seized it." Although he seemed impressed, it was obvious he wasn't completely in agreement with her earlier actions.

"I'm not sure if that's a compliment or an insult," she said laughing.

"To tell ya' the truth, Brigid, I ain't real sure, either," he said laughing. "Let's jes' say it's a compliment and let it go at that."

The two of them continued to chat while they waited. Sheriff Davis told her how things were going for him, and she did the same. Eventually, Brigid spotted something.

"There they are," she said when she saw the white van pull into the same spot where it had been earlier.

"Good eye," he said as he pulled out a pair of binoculars. "Looks like one guy's gettin' out of the van. I think it's still runnin'." He watched for a moment before turning to her and saying, "There's a camera with a decent lens under the seat. See if ya' can get a few photos."

Thankfully, there was a light nearby making it fairly easy for Brigid to see the man as she held the camera up and began to focus.

"That one of 'em?" Corey asked as they both watched.

"Yes," Brigid said, as both men walked to the back of the van with a box. "Those are the two men I saw earlier."

"Good," Sheriff Davis said. "At least there's only two of 'em fer now. Watch 'em as long as you can. I'm gonna' keep my eye on the exit. Looks to me like their gettin' ready to leave again. There's only one way for 'em to come out. We jes' need to see which way they go."

Corey put the binoculars away and started the car. Just then the van backed out of the parking space and drove out of sight behind the building.

"I can't see them anymore," she said.

Corey backed his car out of the space, lights off, and then slowly crept to the exit. Brigid watched as the van appeared at the exit and turned in their direction.

"Lucky break," Corey said as he waited for them to drive past. Brigid snapped a couple of photos as they drove by, making sure to get the front damage as well as the license number. After waiting for a few moments, Corey pulled out, following the van at a reasonable distance.

"There's not much out this way," Brigid pointed out. "Any idea where they could be going?"

Sheriff Davis shook his head as he kept his eye on the van. "Not really. There's a lotta' places they could be usin'. We bust a lot of drug dealers out in this area." While Brigid watched the van, she couldn't help but feel sad as she looked at the darkened buildings they were passing. Every town had its less desirable areas, and Cottonwood Springs was no exception, no matter how much Brigid wished it was.

After a few miles, the buildings got fewer and farther in between, and now they were on an older blacktop road that used to be the main highway before the new interstate had been built.

"There ain't much out this way 'cept farms, forest, and fields," Corey observed. "Maybe we're gonna' get lucky."

"What do you mean?" Brigid asked. The taillights of the van were much farther ahead than she was comfortable with, but Corey didn't seem too concerned.

"Well, sometimes when people are taken, they're held somewhere else. Usually somewhere that no one'll notice 'em comin' and goin' or hear the captives. After all, someone would have probably noticed if they'd dragged Olivia into their hotel room."

Brigid could see his point. It made more sense for them to keep her out here in this remote area. Brigid was glad she had her jacket on, because her blood felt as though it had turned to ice. She couldn't imagine being taken out to the middle of nowhere and locked up in a place so far away from things that you could scream until your voice was gone, and no one would ever hear you.

"Look, they're turnin'," Corey said very quietly, as if the men in the van could hear him.

The road they turned onto was a gravel one, the rocks crunching under the tires. Thankfully there was a slight breeze out of the south, which pushed the dust off the road. Otherwise, as far ahead as they were, Brigid was afraid they would have lost them.

"Do you know where we are?" she asked, suddenly concerned they could be lost. The van turned another corner, and its taillights disappeared.

"Sure do," he said. "Know these roads like the back of my hand." He slowed as the road dipped down, and they went over an old bridge that crossed a small creek. Once they climbed back up on the other side, the van's taillights reappeared.

"Just what is out this way?" she asked.

"Like I said, purty much nothin' 'cept farms, forest, and fields. Most of this is all private land. We won't be able to follow 'em if they turn in somewhere." Brigid could see in the light from the dash that Corey's face was pinched with concentration.

After another couple of miles, the van's brake lights lit up.

"They're slowin' down," he said. "We'll have to drive by when they pull in. It looks like they're drivin' into a field. See if ya' can take any pictures or see anythin' when we go by. Need to find out what they're doin'."

"Got it," Brigid said as she sat up in her seat. She watched as the van pulled off the road ahead of them. There were trees lining the road, but as they drew closer, she saw an opening leading into a field. She began to take photo after photo. She didn't know if any of it would help, but she had to try.

"Looks like an old storage container," she said as she strained her eyes in the darkness. "I can just make it out from their headlights. I think they parked by it."

"Yer' right. That's old man Simmon's property. He'll be in bed by now." Corey drove a bit farther past where the van had turned in before pulling over to the side of the road and shutting off the lights. "Let me see the camera."

Brigid handed it over and he began to cycle through the pictures.

"Yer' right. They're doing somethin' near that storage container."

"Can't we go back there and question them?" Brigid asked. "If it's not their property, then they're trespassing."

"It's not that simple, Brigid," he sighed. "We don't know if they got permission to be there. If they do, and we pull in there, we're the ones trespassin'."

Brigid sat back in her seat and sighed. "So now what?"

"I'll talk to old man Simmons and show him these pictures. If he didn't give 'em permission to be out there, we got probable cause to arrest 'em," he said as he handed the camera back, turned on the headlights, and began to drive.

"And then we come back out here and see what's in the container?" she asked.

"Not quite," he said. "We wanna' catch 'em out here, too. That way there's overwhelmin' evidence against 'em. Ya' also don't want 'em to run if they see us out here. No, we gotta' wait until they come back out here, but when they do, we'll be waitin'."

CHAPTER FIFTEEN

Shortly after Brigid left with Sheriff Davis, Linc turned on the television. He propped his feet up on the coffee table, leaned back, and settled in. It was the only way he knew how to deal with the current situation. He felt anxious about Brigid leaving with Sheriff Davis to hunt down the kidnappers or whatever you wanted to call them, but he also knew she'd be okay.

Sheriff Davis was a good man, and Linc knew he'd do all he could to keep Brigid safe. She was a strong, brave woman, and he had no intention of trying to change that. It was one of the things he loved most about her. She wouldn't change her mind to fit in with what was popular. Instead, she'd voice her opinion and do what she could to make things right. Something his ex-wife had never done.

The house was quiet, and he heard Holly's door when it squeaked open. Apparently, Jett did as well, because his head came up and his tail started thumping. Although her footsteps were muffled, Linc heard her when she entered the room behind where he was sitting. He didn't turn towards her, instead, he chose to let her come to him. He had a feeling something was wrong, but he didn't want to push it.

"Did Brigid leave?" she asked in a voice barely above a whisper.

Linc put the television on mute and turned to face Holly. "Yeah, just a little while ago. Why don't you sit down with me and keep me company?"

Holly slowly walked around the couch and flopped down in an armchair next to the couch. "Is she mad at me?" Her voice was so quiet that Linc could barely hear her. He straightened up and clicked the television off. He wanted to give her his full attention. The movement on the screen was distracting, and he thought this seemed like something that he needed to be fully focused on.

"I don't think so. Why would she be?" he asked gently. He'd never seen Holly look so unsure of herself. It was surprising. He and Holly were usually joking around and having fun, so he wasn't familiar with this part of her.

Holly was hiding her face behind her hair, wringing her hands before she finally started to pick at her nails. "Because I didn't do what she asked me to do. I didn't call her, and she couldn't find me."

Linc heard her sniffle softly and was fairly sure he saw a teardrop fall onto her arm. His heart ached for her. The poor girl had already been through so much. It was no wonder she was worried.

"I think she was more worried than mad, Holly," he said easily. "She's been under a lot of stress lately."

"I know," Holly sighed. "I didn't do it to be a pain." Her voice wobbled as it grew thick with emotion.

"I never thought you did, and I don't think Brigid did, either." Linc was feeling a little out of his depth talking to Holly like this. But then he remembered, this girl was going to be living with him soon. Sure, they got along great, much like an uncle and a niece, but he realized that his role in her life would soon become a little more important than that.

"You know how it is. Sometimes being really worried about someone can make you look like you're mad when in reality, you aren't." He was struggling to think of just the right words to say when Holly broke the silence.

"My mom hit me once," she said, her voice still shaking. She began to pick an almost invisible piece of lint off her pants. "I wasn't home when she expected me to be there. Honestly, I didn't really expect her to be there, either. I guess she'd been sitting at home for a while waiting for me. She was drunk or high or most likely both. I'd gone to the library because it was one of those nights when they show a cartoon for the little kids. It seemed like that was something better to do than sit around all night by myself watching the mice run across the kitchen counter."

Linc started to open his mouth, but on second thought, closed it. He had a feeling Holly needed to get this off her chest. Sometimes the best thing to do for someone is to just listen. Let them get out whatever it is that's weighing them down.

"When I finally got home, she was really worked up. She started screaming at me, asking me where I'd been. I tried explaining to her where I'd been, but I started getting angry too." Holly finally lifted her eyes to meet Linc's. He saw the pain and sadness that was still raw and now on the surface. He realized that the situation earlier that evening had stirred something up in the young girl.

"I yelled at her. I told her if she wasn't such a worthless person, she would have known where her daughter was. That's when she slapped me. Hard. After that she took off again. It was another day or so before I saw her. She didn't even remember coming home," Holly sighed. "She asked me where the bruise came from, so I told her. She shook her head and didn't believe me. She thought I was just kidding or something." Tears welled up in her eyes and slid down her cheeks. "I wasn't lying."

"Come here, Holly," Linc said soothingly. He held his arms out to her, and she rushed over to him. Snuggling up beside him, she began to sob. Linc made soft, calming sounds to her as he slowly rocked her back and forth.

"I didn't mean to upset Brigid," Holly hiccupped.

"I know you didn't. Brigid was just worried, that's all. I'm sure your mom was, too. Sometimes, when people get emotional, they do and say things they don't mean. I'm not saying it was right for your mom to hit you, but you know that doesn't mean she didn't love you, right?" Linc asked as he rubbed her back.

"Yes," she said softly. "Just like I didn't mean to tell her she was a bad mom. She wasn't a great one, by any means, but she still had her good side."

"I'm sure she did," Linc reassured. "We all have good sides and bad sides. Unfortunately, I think your mom carried a lot of hurt around inside her, and she tried to numb it with alcohol and drugs. A lot of people do that, actually. They can't handle certain things in their life, so they try to shut them away."

"You think?" Holly asked as she sat up and wiped her eyes.

"I'm sure of it. You'd be surprised. Now, that doesn't give them a right to do what they do. After all, everyone has problems, but sometimes people don't understand they need to face them rather than hide from them. Then, when they try to quit all those things they've been trying to hide from, they come at them full force. That's when they relapse."

Linc hadn't known Holly's mother personally, but he did have a few friends in his life that he'd lost to addiction. He knew that addicts were just people like everyone else, a little lost and broken, feeling like they had nothing to live for, and overwhelmed by their past actions.

"Do you think my mom would have relapsed?" she asked, her eyes wide.

In that moment, Linc was struck by just how young Holly was. Sure, she was a bright teenage girl who had seen and lived with so much in her short life. But she also was just a young girl with all the insecurities and struggles of a typical teenager.

"No, I don't think she would have," he said after a moment.

"Why?" she asked curiously.

"Because she had a good reason not to," he explained. "She had you."

"She had me before and that didn't stop her," Holly said, her face becoming dark.

"That's true. But Brigid told me about her and how determined she was to make things right between the two of you. I think that's got to count for something." Linc watched as a thread of hope brightened Holly's face. They lapsed into silence. Linc allowed her time to think, knowing she was probably working through some important stuff in her head at that moment.

"If Brigid isn't mad at me, then why did she leave? Why are you here?"

Linc suddenly realized what had triggered all of this. She thought Brigid left just like her mother did the night she hit her.

"She left because they think they may have found the people who took Olivia. You know how Brigid is, she likes to be involved. When Sheriff Davis said he was going to go stake out the van that took Olivia, she volunteered to go with him. Did you know she went and knocked on their motel room door and was face to face with those guys?"

Linc was still in shock over the whole thing. When he'd heard what she'd done, he wasn't sure if he wanted to strangle her or hold her. Not that he would ever lay a hand on her, but it had terrified him so much he'd had the urge to shake some sense into her. Of course, that still probably wouldn't stop her.

"Are you serious? She could have gotten hurt!" Holly exclaimed.

"I know. But do you want to know why I think she did it?" he asked.

Holly didn't say anything, just listened intently.

"I think she did it because she wants to make sure you, and everyone else, is safe. She may not fully realize that's why she's doing it, but I'd bet that's the reason behind it. Brigid likes to take care of people. That's who she is. She'd give someone the shirt off her back if she thought they needed it. There's no way she can just sit back and not help when she knows something needs to be done. It's one of the things I love about her." Linc couldn't help but smile as he felt the love he had for Brigid expand in his chest.

"She is pretty amazing," Holly finally said. "So you don't think she's going to make me leave? She's not going to make me move to Missouri or go into foster care?"

"Never," Linc said. "She loves you like family. Just because you two aren't blood related doesn't mean she doesn't love you like you are. Things will get bumpy once in a while, but that's life. Just always try to communicate, and I think all three of us will do alright together."

Holly nodded. "Okay, I can do that. And I promise I'll take what she says to heart a little more next time. I wasn't thinking, that's all. I didn't realize she'd get so upset."

"I know, and I'm sure she does, too. But I think when you get a chance, you should tell her so yourself. Just to clear the air and make sure everyone's on the same page."

"I will. When do you think she'll get back?" she asked.

"I'm not sure. That's why I was hanging out here with you. I didn't want you to be all by yourself." He leaned over and bumped her shoulder with his.

"Thanks, Linc. I appreciate it," she said softly.

"Hey, you want to make some peanut butter cookies?" he asked.

"Do you even need to ask? You know how I love those cookies of yours. I love late night snacks," she said grinning.

"That's my girl," he said as he stood up. "I'll go see if Brigid has the ingredients I need for them. If not, I've got them at my house. Then we can binge watch some television until she gets back."

CHAPTER SIXTEEN

Sheriff Davis dropped Brigid off assuring her he'd get in touch the following afternoon to let her know what he learned about the property where the men they'd followed had gone. Even though he was pretty sure he knew whose property it was, he still had to make certain and then get in contact with the owner. He made her promise to get lots of rest and to think about something besides the Oliva Ford case for a while.

When she unlocked her front door, she was eagerly greeted by Jett, who was obviously happy she was home. "Hey boy," she said as she scratched his ears. He leaned against her, letting her know in dog language that he was happy to see her.

She glanced over at the couch and smiled when she saw Linc and Holly sound asleep. Linc had his feet on the coffee table, his head tipped back, and was softly snoring. Holly was curled up next to him, her head on his shoulder. The remains of a plate of peanut butter cookies were on the table in front of them.

Brigid crept as quietly as she could over to them and gingerly lifted the remote from Linc's hand. Clicking it off, she turned, and touched his leg. "Linc?" she said softly.

His eyes opened slowly and it took him a moment to collect himself and remember where he was. "Hey," he said sleepily.

Noticing that Holly was asleep on him, he carefully slipped out from underneath her, lowering her as gently as possible onto the couch. "What time is it?" he asked Brigid.

"I don't know. Late," she said. "You didn't have to stay."

"I know," he said, "but I wanted to." He turned and looked over at Holly. Tugging a throw blanket from the back of the couch, he covered her, then he turned back to Brigid and waved her towards the kitchen.

Once they were in the kitchen, he leaned against the counter. "Holly was pretty upset earlier."

"Really? About what?" Brigid asked.

"She thought that since she hadn't done what you asked, that you'd kick her out," he said. "She thought you left because of her."

"I didn't," she protested.

"I know," he said softly. "And I told her that. She told me about some stuff that happened with her mom a while back, and the whole situation kind of stirred things up for her. She's okay now, but maybe you could spend a little time with her tomorrow morning. Just the two of you? No work or investigating cases or anything. Just two pretty ladies doing something fun together," he suggested.

"Sure," Brigid said, surprised. "I didn't even think she was upset when I left."

"I wondered," Linc admitted. "But I didn't want you to worry. I want you to know I have your back. We're going to be a family. I don't want it to be an us versus them sort of thing. I want all of us to work together so we understand one another. That's why I stepped in. She's a smart girl, and with everything she's been through, it's easy to forget that she's just a kid."

"That it is," Brigid agreed. "Thank you." She yawned loudly. "I'm sorry," she whispered. "I'm just exhausted."

"I need to go anyway. Get some sleep. We'll talk more tomorrow." Linc kissed Brigid on the forehead as he pulled her in for a hug. "I love you."

"I love you, too," Brigid said as she smiled. "Thanks for just being you."

"It's my pleasure," he said as he released her.

"I'm going to visit a woman tomorrow about our cake. She runs a bakery business out of her house, and I hear she does really great work," Brigid said as she kicked her shoes off. "You want to come?"

"I could…," Linc began and then he stopped, "but why don't you take Holly? I still have work to do, and you know I like any and all cakes. I'm not going to be too worried about what you pick out. You two go and enjoy yourself. Maybe do a little shopping while you're at it."

"That does sound like fun," Brigid admitted.

"Hey, you're home," a scratchy voice called from the couch. Brigid and Linc turned to see Holly sitting up.

"Yeah, sorry if we woke you," Brigid said as they returned to the great room.

"Not a problem," Holly said, stretching. "Look, I'm really sorry about this afternoon, Brigid."

"Don't worry about it," Brigid said as she sat down next to her. "You won't do it again, will you?"

Holly shook her head emphatically. "Not a chance."

"Then I think we're good. Hey, you want to go try some wedding cake tasting with me tomorrow morning? Maybe go shopping or do something after that?" Brigid asked as she brushed Holly's hair back from her face.

"Free cake? I'm all in," she said smiling. Suddenly, she reached out and wrapped her arms around Brigid, hugging her tightly. "I love you, Brigid."

"I love you too, Holly," Brigid said feeling a little emotional. A lump began to form in her throat as she hugged her back. "You better get to bed. I don't want you grumpy in the morning." She patted her on the back.

"Okay, good night," Holly said as she stood up and waved to them.

"Good night," Brigid said.

"Night," Linc called.

"Oh, and Linc?" Holly said as she paused just inside the hall.

"What's up?" he said.

"Thanks for our little talk. I love you, too," she said with a small smile.

"Love you too, kiddo. You have fun tomorrow." Linc's voice was thick with emotion as Holly turned and stepped into her bedroom.

"Did that get you right in the feels?" Brigid asked with a small tear in her eye.

"You bet it did," he said exhaling loudly. "I'm heading home. Talk to you tomorrow." He gave her a kiss and walked out the door.

As Brigid was walking down the hall to her room, she thought about what Linc had said. He was right. She'd been treating Holly almost like a roommate. Not that it was a bad thing, but maybe, just maybe that wasn't what she really needed right now. She probably needed to know what having a loving and caring parent was like, and apparently Linc was intuitive enough to have seen that.

She changed her clothes and washed her face, thinking how lucky she was. Linc was an amazing man who was wise beyond his years, but also young at heart. Holly was brilliant, but also extremely caring. She listened and always tried to help, a rare thing in a teenager. Brigid realized she was a truly blessed woman to have developed a relationship with these two amazing and caring individuals.

As she got in bed and pulled the blankets up to her chin, Brigid couldn't help but smile thinking of all the wonderful people she had in her life. It was terrifying to think people could just vanish into thin air. Of course, she knew that wasn't literally what had happened, but it still seemed that way. One minute, Olivia Ford had been picking a few things up at the grocery store. The next minute, she was missing. Gone, almost without a trace. If it hadn't been for the security cameras, they would have zero leads to work with.

Brigid knew it was easy to sit in the safety of her home and think something like that would never happen to her. The reality of it was far too scary to think about. Every day, all across the country, people disappeared. Some, never to be heard from again. Granted, not all of them were kidnapped or sold into human trafficking, but a lot of them were.

Since learning about what happened to Olivia, Brigid had done a quick research on the topic of missing people. She'd read that over 3,000 people were sold or kidnapped into slavery every day. That number had been a real eye opener. That was like the population of a small town just, poof, disappearing every day. Some of them would be lucky and get rescued, but so many others wouldn't be as lucky.

She'd learned that between 600,000 to 800,000 people were trafficked across international borders every year. Around 80% of them were female and many were children. It was simply incomprehensible to Brigid.

Her heart ached for every single person in the world who was living in slavery. The website she'd visited had said the majority of those taken were forced into prostitution. She couldn't wrap her mind around that thought. Who could do that to another human being? What kind of a world did we live in where this was a very real danger we had to worry about?

Sitting up in bed, Brigid felt compelled to bow her head. She wasn't exactly the praying type, but now she felt the need. It wasn't that she wasn't religious. It was more that she just hadn't thought about it in a long time. As she folded her hands and closed her eyes, her thoughts were focused on all the people who had been taken from their families and forced into servitude.

"God, please help the people who have been taken from their loved ones. Please, help them find their way home. People like Olivia Ford don't deserve to be taken away from their homes and loved ones and then forced into slavery. Help us bring her home."

She remained with her head bowed for several long moments, thinking positive thoughts that they would find Olivia. She didn't know if her small prayer would help, but it was the only thing she could think of to try and get through this ordeal. There was no way she'd be able to sleep if she was afraid they wouldn't be able to bring Olivia home.

She sighed deeply, and slid back down under her blankets. For now, her loved ones were safe, but she was faced with a sleepless night of tossing and turning.

CHAPTER SEVENTEEN

The next day, Brigid and Holly had a leisurely, relaxing morning. They were to meet Lewellen around 10:00 a.m. to taste her various types of cakes, so there was no need to rush around. Brigid enjoyed sitting on the patio and sipping her coffee with Holly while they listened to the birds chirping and watched Jett chasing squirrels.

"I'm really sorry I didn't do like you told me to do," Holly finally said. She'd been struggling to find the right words all morning.

"I know," Brigid said thoughtfully. "I realize you've practically had to raise yourself, so it may seem to go against what you're used to. For the most part, I trust you to make the right decisions. After all, you've done a good job of keeping yourself out of trouble so far." Brigid took another sip of her coffee, using it as a chance to think about her next words. "I just want you to trust that if I tell you I want you to do something, I have a reason for it."

"I understand," Holly whispered as she lowered her head.

"You're not in trouble," Brigid said as she softly touched Holly's shoulder. "You just didn't understand. It was a miscommunication between us. I see it as an opportunity for us to learn a little more about each other and work out the kinks. That's all."

Holly lifted her head and looked hopefully at her informal

guardian. "You don't want me to move out?"

"Are you kidding?" Brigid scoffed. "It never even crossed my mind. Look, we can disagree about things, but that doesn't mean I want you to leave. I know there are going to be times we don't see eye to eye, but I'll never tell you to move out. You're already like a daughter to me. I care about you a lot, Holly. I won't ever give up on you."

Holly broke into a wide grin. "Thank you. I know we talked about it last night but…," she let her sentence trail off.

"You wanted to make sure everything was still the same this morning. I get it," Brigid nodded. "It is, don't worry." Remembering she still hadn't mentioned it to Holly she cried "Oh! I almost forgot. I wanted to ask you to be a bridesmaid with Missy. Fiona is going to be the matron of honor."

"Are you serious?" Holly exclaimed.

"Completely. What do you say? We can look at dresses online if you'd like? Or I can take you to the dress shop where I got the other dresses?"

"Let's look online," Holly nodded. "Now I'm really excited."

"Good. That means a lot to me." She looked at her watch and sighed, "We should probably get ready to go. It's about that time."

They went inside, leaving Jett to play in the backyard while they were gone. Brigid picked up her purse from the hall table and they walked out to her car, ready to cake-test at Lewellen's home.

"I never realized so many people had businesses in their own homes," Holly said.

"It's a lot cheaper," Brigid answered. "You don't have to pay rent and you can set your own hours, plus you don't have to leave your home. I think it's wonderful Lewellen has been able to do something like this from her home. It's kind of a natural, plus I hear that commercial kitchens are really expensive to build."

A few minutes later, Brigid drove into the driveway of a small one-story ranch style home with a sign in the yard that had "Lewellen's Cakes" written on it. Brigid put the car in park and they climbed out.

"You must be Brigid," a plump older woman said as she emerged through the front door, smiling. Her reddish blonde hair looked as though it was freshly curled, and she had an apron tied around her thick waist.

"Yes, ma'am," Brigid said as they shook hands. "This is Holly. I brought her along to help me decide what I should order."

"Nice to meet you Holly," Lewellen said as she shook her hand. "Well let's get in the house and get you started trying out some of my cakes."

They followed her inside and back to a kitchen which was in the rear of the house and quite professional looking with a round table and chairs nearby. Lewellen motioned for them to sit down at the table as she headed to the far counter.

"I made a few different kinds of cakes into cupcakes. Obviously, we can mix and match icings and such. I just put together the usual combinations, so you could try a variety of them out. And don't worry, I have plain frosting in the refrigerator if you want to try it by itself," Lewellen said as she carried a tray of cupcakes to them and set it on the table.

"This has got to be one of the best days ever," muttered Holly as her eyes grew wider and wider as she looked at the display in front of her.

"Like cupcakes, do you?" Lewellen asked with a chuckle. Holly nodded vigorously. "Then it's a good thing Brigid brought you. Sometimes brides can get tired of all the sweets, and they have a really hard time making a decision."

"There's no way that's happening with me. I could eat cupcakes every day," Holly said as she rubbed her hands together in anticipation, a glazed look in her eyes.

Lewellen began showing them the different flavors and explained what each one was and the flavors she felt would complement each one. They talked about fillings and icing and colors. Brigid had never really put too much thought into what the options were for a wedding cake. Things had changed so much since she was first married when it was common to only do things that were traditional. White cake with white icing and things like that. She'd never even dreamed of being able to have different kinds of fillings and frostings on a wedding cake.

"I don't know how I'm ever going to be able to choose one over the others," she finally said after she'd tried her sixth cupcake. She was only trying a small sample of each, while Holly eagerly took far more enthusiastic bite size samples.

"May I make a suggestion?" Lewellen asked. "Narrow it down slowly. First, eliminate what you know you don't want." She stood up and walked over to the refrigerator where there was a large binder sitting on top of it. She pulled it down and took a slip of paper out before handing it to Brigid.

On it, there were all the different flavors of cakes, icings, and possible fillings. "Cross off any you know you don't want. Then, think about the ones you do like. If you want to have one with a filling, you're a little more limited on the designs you can choose, because I don't like to make a tall cake with a filling. The fillings tend to make the cake unstable. Don't want the cake to fall on top of you and ruin your wedding dress," she chuckled.

"That makes complete sense," Brigid said nodding. "Thank you. Your cakes are amazing, and I definitely want to hire you to make the wedding cake. I just need a little time to think about what I want."

"That's not a problem," Lewellen said as she sat back down. "May I ask you a quick question?"

"Of course," Brigid said. She looked over at Holly who was playing on her phone while she took bites of the different cupcakes.

"I heard Olivia Ford is missing, and you're helping the sheriff find her. Is that true?" she asked in a hushed tone, as if there were other people present who might overhear her.

"Word travels fast," Brigid said. "Yes, it's true, but I'm not working in an official capacity or anything like that. I just help question people and dig up information while the law enforcement officials deal with the crime scene and things like that."

"Amazing," Lewellen said, mystified. "I've also heard you've helped the sheriff's department with a few other cases as well. When I heard about Olivia, my heart dropped. She's such a good person and has such a big heart. I hope and pray you'll find her, and she'll be alright. I know her husband is sick with worry, as we all are."

"We are too," Brigid said softly. "We're making progress, but when it comes to finding evidence and building a case that will stand up in court, it takes time."

"I'm sure that's true," she said nodding. "You probably need to be certain you're covering all your bases, so someone doesn't end up walking free on a technicality."

"Exactly," Brigid said.

"Any idea what's going on? I heard about a young boy going missing a few towns over about a week ago. Do you think they're connected?" she asked.

Brigid knew they were getting into touchy territory. She wanted to make sure she didn't say anything she shouldn't, so she decided to deflect the question. "I'm not really sure at this point. I don't have all the information myself. I just give the sheriff the information I come up with and let him put the pieces together. I don't have the connections and the contacts he does."

"Right, right. That makes sense," Lewellen said nodding.

"As for the cake and everything," Brigid said, "I'll contact you when I make a final decision. I'm pretty sure I emailed you the date and the location of the wedding, correct?" Brigid was starting to lose track of who she'd told what to.

"Yes, you have. There's no hurry. I just like to know a week before the wedding what I'm going to be making, so I'll be sure I have everything I need to prepare it. Think about it. What selection do you think you're going to make? Do you have a few that you're trying to decide between? I can send some more samples of those if you want to talk with your fiancé about them." Lewellen stood up and went over to a cabinet and pulled down a collapsed and folded flat bakery box.

"Yes, that would be fabulous. I'm really trying to decide between these four right here," Brigid said as she showed Lewellen the list.

"Is the devil's food on there with the cherry filling?" Holly asked, looking up from her phone. "Personally, I think that's the best."

I'll tell you what," Lewellen said as she built the box and began to place cupcakes inside. "I'll add a couple of those just for you Miss Holly."

"Thank you," Holly said, "but you don't have to do that."

"Oh, pish posh," Lewellen scoffed. "I know how teenagers are. You'll eat them, won't you?" she asked.

Holly nodded enthusiastically. "You can count on it."

That's all I want, then. My grandkids usually help polish off any extras I have, but they're all busy right now. You take them. My treat." She placed the extra cupcakes inside the box and closed it before handing it to Holly.

"Thank you so much," Brigid said. "You're too kind."

"It's no trouble. Let me know if I can do anything else for you."

Brigid and Holly said their goodbyes before heading out to the car. As Brigid was buckling up, she looked over and saw that Holly was already eating one of the extra cupcakes.

"How can you eat that many cupcakes and not have an upset stomach?" Brigid asked in wonder.

"Just lucky, I guess," Holly said as Brigid backed out of the driveway.

"Well don't spoil your lunch. Remember, we're going shopping and out to lunch. You can pick the place."

"Best. Day. Ever," Holly said as they drove away.

"Where to first? Should we see what they have at the antique mall? I know how much you love looking at all kinds of stuff," Brigid said. "Maybe they'll still have that antique writing desk you liked so much last time."

"Do you think?" Holly asked. "Although, I don't know what I'd use it for."

"Okay, we could go somewhere else. Maybe go try that new restaurant in Great Bend?" Brigid suggested.

"Oh, that sounds great. I heard they have really great pizza," Holly said.

"How can you possibly still be thinking about eating?" Brigid asked in amazement. "I was kind of thinking a little later."

"Oh, well, I am a growing girl, you know. I need all my vitamins and minerals," she said beaming.

"You are one goofy kid, you know that?" Brigid said with a laugh.

"Yeah, I know," Holly said proudly.

CHAPTER EIGHTEEN

That evening, Linc came over to Brigid's for dinner, and she prepared a warm steak salad which Linc and Holly both declared was the best salad they'd ever had. They loved the addition of cherries to complement the steak with arugula. Brigid thought she might have to leave and go with Sheriff Davis, so they were eating earlier than they normally ate. She'd been anxiously awaiting a call from him.

"Calm down, honey," Linc said as Brigid paced and fidgeted with various things around the kitchen. She'd only picked at her dinner, barely able to eat.

"I'm trying," she admitted. "It's just I'm surprised I haven't heard from him yet. I'm worried something's wrong."

"I'm sure he'll call soon," Linc said trying to console her. "Didn't you say you had some cupcakes from this morning for me to try?"

"Oh, yes," Brigid said as she hurried over to the refrigerator. She slid the box out and carried it over to the table. Just then her phone began to ring, and as she picked it up off the counter, she saw it was the sheriff.

She said, "Hello?" as Holly began to point out to Linc all the different cupcake flavors and explain about each one.

"Hey, Brigid, it's Corey. I've been runnin' around like crazy today, but I finally got some news fer you."

"Great, I've been getting antsy," she said chuckling.

"I'll bet, and I apologize. It seemed everybody and their brother was havin' troubles today. My deputies and me been runnin' all over the county. I found out those men we saw last night don't have permission to be on that property. When I told old man Simmons he had some guys pokin' around on his land and they may be storin' stuff in that shippin' container of his, he went ballistic. Used some mighty colorful language, but long story short, he wants 'em arrested," Sheriff Davis explained.

"Well, that's great. Isn't it?" Brigid asked.

"It is. Know it may seem I'm being overly cautious," he began, but Brigid cut him off.

"No, I understand. If these guys are really into what you think, we don't want to let them get away," Brigid insisted.

"Exactly. If they're part of some sort of human traffickin' ring, we can't let 'em slip through our fingers. Who knows how many other people they may have hurt before or could hurt in the future? I'm worried about Olivia and her unborn baby, but I gotta' keep everyone else in mind, too."

He sighed so deeply it sounded as though it was coming from the depths of his soul. "You know, murder investigations are one thing. But this, this is another level. This is my best friend's wife. Could even be my godchild."

"I thought about that too," Brigid said, "but their lives aren't already lost. We just don't know what's happening out there." She knew the weariness that Sheriff Davis was experiencing, but for her, that feeling manifested as nervous energy.

"That's right. And I'm sittin' here wonderin' if I'm takin' too long to get to the bottom of it. So help me, if anythin' happens to her, I'll never forgive myself."

"You can't think like that, Corey" Brigid said, trying to console him. "You have to believe you'll find her, and she'll be okay."

"Yeah, yer' right. That's what I like about ya', Brigid. Ya' help me keep things in perspective," Corey said sounding a little more optimistic.

"So, what's the plan?" Brigid asked.

"I've had a coupla' deputies watchin' the container since around 8:00 this mornin'. So far, nobody's gone out there. Don't know if we spooked 'em or if they're just bein' careful. Either way, I thought you and me could take the watch tonight. Ol' man Simmons says there's a huntin' blind in the treeline right near there. He says it's good size and solid, so it'd be a good place to get a better view of 'em if they come back," he explained.

"That sounds like a good plan. You can arrest them for trespassing and then see what's going on in that storage container." Brigid liked the plan. A hunting blind would allow them to blend in much better than sitting in a parked vehicle. Even out in the country that could raise suspicions. They wouldn't want anyone to think they were just having problems with their car and stop to help. While that was usually a good thing in this area, it could completely blow their cover tonight.

"Ya' got it," Sheriff Davis said. "We'll take one of them unmarked sheriff trucks, so we can pull out into the field on the other side and hide it. I was thinkin' of headin' out there in about thirty minutes. If yer' free, I'll swing by and pick ya' up."

"I wouldn't miss it," Brigid said as she turned and looked at Holly and Linc sampling cupcakes.

"Good, and Brigid? If ya' got some sort of a gun or somethin', I want ya' to bring it. I'll do all I can to keep ya' safe, but I like to have multiple contingencies in place. If these guys get violent and somethin' happens to me, I wanna' make sure ya' got a way to protect yerself."

"I hear you. I'll see what I've got," Brigid said before hanging up.

"What's going on?" Linc asked when she returned to the table.

"That was Corey. He wants me to go with him to the stakeout where we saw the men last night. He said they don't have permission to be on that property, and the plan is to arrest them for trespassing, and then see if we can find out what else they're doing after they're in custody. Only thing is, he wants me to bring a gun or something for protection."

Linc knew how Brigid felt about guns. She wasn't a big fan of guns, although she'd gotten a little more comfortable with them over time. She was starting to view them as something of a necessary evil. While they could cause problems, if they were used correctly, they could also help bring things to a safe and quick end.

"Well, you could use mine again?" he suggested. "You're already familiar with it, and you're a good shot. I agree with Corey. It never hurts to make sure you're well protected."

"I know, but Corey will be with me," she began.

"But what if something happens to him, Brigid?" Holly interjected. "You don't want to rely solely on him and then, for whatever reason, he's suddenly unable to protect you. What would Linc and I do if these guys took you, too?" The girl's concern was written all over her face.

"I know," Brigid began. "But..."

"No, buts," Linc interrupted. "I'll run home and get it. I'd rather you take it and not need it, than find yourself in a bad situation and wish you had it." He stood up and hurried out the door with the promise he'd be right back.

"He's right, you know," Holly said. She ran her finger along the side of the cupcake she was working on, swiping off some frosting. "You just never know what these guys may have done, and what they're capable of doing. I mean, think about it. They stole a woman in broad daylight. That's pretty bold."

"You're right," Brigid said as she held up her hands. "I should never assume everything will turn out okay. That's not a very good example to set."

Holly looked surprised that Brigid agreed so readily. "That's right," she finally said. "I need you to be around for a long time."

Brigid smiled. "And why's that?"

"Because I'm going to need somewhere to go when I need a break from college. A place I can go home to. Maybe even call when I get homesick?" she said as she gave Brigid a sideways look.

"That sounds nice," Brigid said. "You might want someone to come visit you, too. Let you know you need to clean your dorm room." Brigid raised her eyebrow and gave Holly a pointed look.

Holly laughed. "They're just clothes. All I have to do is put them away."

"Then you shouldn't have any trouble having it done by tomorrow morning. I don't know how late I'll be tonight, so I don't want you staying up." While she waited for Linc to return, she started cleaning off the kitchen counter and loading the dishwasher. She knew the house wouldn't clean itself while she was gone.

"I have a report due tomorrow, so I should probably get it finished first, and then I'll clean my room." Holly stood and went over to Brigid, then looked at her with a solemn expression. "Promise me you'll be careful?"

"I will," Brigid said as she turned away from her to clean the sink.

"Say it," Holly insisted. Brigid's first instinct was to balk, but when she saw the sincerity in the girl's eyes, she knew this was important to Holly.

"I promise to be careful," Brigid recited.

"And that you'll be here in the morning?" Holly pressed.

Brigid opened her mouth to object and then caught herself. "I'll be here in the morning. Wild horses couldn't keep me from being here for you tomorrow," Brigid promised.

"Good," Holly said as she wrapped her arms around Brigid. "That's what I wanted to hear." She said goodnight and headed off to her room.

Brigid watched Holly as she walked down the hall, Jett following her. She was so very proud of Holly and her big heart, it nearly brought a tear to her eye.

She continued cleaning as she waited for Linc to return. Not only did it give her something to do, but she was also able to burn off some nervous energy. Her mind raced with the possibilities. Everything that could happen, had happened, and so on, continued to race through her mind. By the time Linc returned, she'd already finished with the kitchen and had begun fluffing the throw pillows on the couch.

He tucked the gun in her purse before moving over to her. "Are you nervous?"

"A little," she admitted.

"You know, you don't have to do this," he reminded her. "You can leave the law enforcement work to the professionals." He rubbed her arms lovingly.

"I know that's an option, but I don't think I could live with myself if I did. I know I'm no professional, but I feel like I really make a difference when I help. Corey and his deputies have more than just this case to work on. There are always accidents, things getting stolen, and people needing to be pulled over. They have a lot on their plate. I feel better knowing that I can help them out. I can't imagine turning my back on it all," Brigid admitted.

"So, what's the problem?" Linc asked. "Why are you so jittery?"

"I think it's the not knowing," she said. "I'm kind of ready to put this one behind me."

"I can understand that," he said. "I saw Mike Ford at the bank today. The guy's a wreck, not that I blame him. He told me Corey had said you were helping him, and Mike wanted me to thank you."

"I hope his thanks are warranted," Brigid said. "I just want to find Olivia."

"I know you do," Linc said, "but please understand that Holly and I want you to be safe. No crazy stunts, okay? I'm going to be worried the whole time you're gone. I'm staying right here until you come home."

"You don't have to do that," Brigid said gently touching his face. "I'll be fine, really."

"I don't care," he said. "I won't get a wink of sleep knowing you're out there. At least here, I'll know when you come home and that you're safe. I have my laptop in the truck. I'll bring it in the house and do some work to pass the time."

Brigid smiled, thinking how incredibly grateful she was for this man who had showed up in her life. "Thank you," she said simply.

"No thanks necessary, sweetheart," he said. "I love you more than my next breath. Without you in my life, I'd be a mess."

They stayed in a long hug until a knock at the door let them know Sheriff Corey Davis arrived.

CHAPTER NINETEEN

Sheriff Davis drove them to the rural area where they'd followed the men the previous night. It was still slightly light out as they approached the area, making it look completely different than it had the night before.

"Do you think they'll come back tonight?" Brigid asked as they drew closer.

"Sure hope so," Sheriff Davis replied. "We kept eyes on the area all day, and ain't no one been spotted yet." He slowed the truck down as they passed by the field in question. The shipping container was there, painted red, but fading with rust spots covering it. The grass around it was tall, almost waist high. The area was hilly and inhospitable. She could see why the men had picked the location. If you wanted to hide something, this would be a perfect spot.

Sheriff Davis turned off the road and pulled up in front of a green metal gate. "I got the keys, so we can pull in and hide a bit better. One sec," he said as he hopped out of the truck. Brigid watched as he unlocked the gate and undid the chain that held it in place. He pushed the gate wide open before climbing back in the truck. "Way I see it, they won't be expectin' anyone to be around and they might jes' let their guard down."

"Let's hope so," Brigid said as they pulled through the gate.

Corey climbed back out of the truck, returned to the gate and closed it, wrapping the chain back around and playing with the lock. Finally, he climbed back in the truck. "Jes' so you know, I didn't lock the padlock. Made it look like it is, jes' in case they look over and notice, but I didn't wanna' lock it in case of an emergency."

"Good thinking," Brigid said, nodding as they bumped along through the grass and circled around behind the treeline that was fairly close to the storage container. They didn't go far before Corey pulled up so close to the trees that they were reaching over the truck. Looking out of the window, Brigid noticed the grass on this side of the treeline was much taller. It was almost up to the windows.

"Try not to disturb the grass when ya' get out," Sheriff Davis said. "We wanna' try to leave the area as normal lookin' as possible, but I'd bet they won't come here until it gets dark. This being a black truck and the underbrush bein' so thick, don't think they'll notice anythin' unusual. Still, it's better to be cautious."

Brigid nodded, and they climbed out of the truck. The tall weeds brushed against Brigid, rustling slightly in the breeze. There were no city sounds, and it was extremely quiet. She heard cattle mooing and bawling in the distance. She reached into her purse and pulled out the pistol Linc had put in there, snug in its clip-on holster. She clipped it over the waistband of her jeans before quietly closing the door and carefully making her way around the truck. Sheriff Davis was waiting for her.

"Jes' inside these trees is the blind. I came out here earlier to make sure it'd work. Follow me." He pushed aside a small sapling and began to pick a trail through the underbrush. Brigid was glad she hadn't worn her best clothes. Thorns and sticks poked her as she pressed through, snagging her clothes and hair. As they continued, she felt they were making a lot of noise compared to the quiet around them.

After she took a few more steps she saw a small building in front of them. It appeared to be made from some sort of plywood and painted in greens, greys, and blacks to make it blend in with its surroundings. It was just on the edge of the opposite side of the trees.

"Is that it?" she asked.

"Sure is. Actually, it's one of the nicer blinds I've ever been in. There's even a floor in there." As they got closer, Brigid saw the floor set into the back of it. When they got to the door, Sheriff Davis pulled it open. "Ladies first," he said.

Brigid stepped inside. "You're right, Corey, it is pretty nice, not that I've been in any hunting blinds like this before," she admitted. "What's the point to all this?" She looked around at the bare wood interior and tried to make sense of it. Along the back was a built-in wooden bench, worn from people sitting on it. On the other side was a rectangular opening with netting hanging down. Only the top was attached, leaving it hanging like a curtain that just barely made it down past the window.

"Hunters use blinds so the animals can't see 'em. Some guys use tree stands which are like seats that attach high up in a tree. Others use blinds like this. Most of the time they ain't this well built. A lot of 'em are jes' tents or somethin' like that. Somebody put a lot of time and effort into buildin' this one," he said as he looked around.

"What's with the window and the netting?" Brigid asked as she sat down on the bench.

"The window is so you can see yer' prey. I suppose they put the nettin' up to make it harder to see inside. They'd jes' lift it up when they're aimin'

their gun at their target," he explained.

"Interesting," Brigid said. "Seems like a lot goes into hunting. More than I'd ever expected."

"Ya'd be surprised," he chuckled. "Some guys get real serious about it."

"I can tell," she said. "So what do we do now?"

"Fer right now, we wait. I suspect they'll come after full dark like they done last night. I gotta' make sure they pull up in the field and are fully on the property before I can do anythin'. I gotta' ask you a question. How sure of yerself are you with that gun?" he asked as he nodded toward the pistol on her hip.

"I've gone to the gun range off and on with it," she said. "Linc likes to make sure I can hit something with it."

"Well, I seen ya' use a gun once, and you was purty good. Don't mean to be rude, but if yer' my partner at the moment, I jes' wanna' make sure yer' good. Don't mean nothin' personal," he said. Brigid couldn't blame him. He probably wanted to make sure he wasn't going to end up getting accidently shot in the process.

"I'm sure I'm good enough to hit someone at this distance, if need be," she said as she looked out the window towards the storage container.

"Then that's good enough fer me," he said as he followed her line of sight. "Thinkin' is I come up on one side of the container, and ya' come up on the other. I'll make myself known first, so if they got weapons, they'll fire on me. I got a coupla' deputies who are close by if we need 'em. The truck ain't exactly made for takin' suspects into custody."

Brigid nodded. "So they're just waiting for your signal to swoop in and help clean up the mess?"

"Purty much," he said laughing. "But for now, we jes' gonna' havta' wait."

"I can do that. Thought we might have a little dead time, so I brought a snack for us, butterscotch bars. Here, take one," she said, pulling two out of her pocket.

"Man, that's an added bonus to the night," Corey said as he

finished the brownie. "Ya' can bring them along anytime we got a stakeout."

"Corey, let's think positive. Let's think we only got to have these tonight, because we won't be back for any more stakeouts. We're going to get them tonight."

"Like the way ya' think, girl."

CHAPTER TWENTY

The sun had fully set when Brigid spotted headlights coming down the road. They weren't moving very fast, and Sheriff Davis doubted that it was them.

"They was drivin' faster than that last night. That's probably just someone headin' home late from work," he grumbled.

"I don't know, Corey, I think it may be them," Brigid muttered as they watched the lights approaching. Sure enough, they slowed even more as they approached the field.

"It's show time," Sheriff Davis said as he reached for his gun. Sitting on the edge of the bench, he waited, and watched.

The white van pulled in, bumping over clumps of grass and the rough ground of the field. It finally came to a stop with its headlights shining directly on the side of the storage container. Brigid held her breath as she watched, her eyes straining to see past the bright headlights.

Both doors of the van opened and two men got out. Brigid recognized them as being the same two she'd seen at the motel the previous day. She heard the men speaking to each other in low tones. As they approached the storage container, Sheriff Davis motioned to Brigid that they were going to make their move. Silently, they crept out of the hunting blind and through the grass.

Brigid slipped her gun from the holster on her belt and clicked the safety off. She was sure the men would be able to hear her heart beating even though she was quite a distance from them. It was hard work keeping her breath slow and steady. Every nerve in her body wanted to start screaming in panic, but she resisted the urge and silently moved forward. Her thoughts raced as she wondered if she was really a good enough shot to be of any use, but it was too late to change her mind.

Corey motioned for her to go around the other side of the container and they split up. Brigid kept the metal wall right next to her as she slowly took long steps, hoping that they couldn't hear the extra rustling through the grass. The sound of it brushing up against her would surely give her away.

However, they didn't seem to notice. They continued to mumble to each other, but Brigid's blood was rushing in her ears too loudly to focus on what they were saying. She heard the rattle of keys and the sound of a metal padlock being opened. Then she heard Sheriff Davis bellow, "Freeze, Sheriff's Department!"

Brigid stepped away from the safety of the storage container and assumed a two-handed shooting stance with her gun pointed at the two men. Both turned in her direction, no doubt contemplating running. When they saw her step into the light, they both raised their hands, but one of them took off in the only direction left, behind them. Just as quickly, Sheriff Davis fired, shooting the man in the leg. Crying out in pain, he hit the ground, clutching his leg where he'd been shot.

"105 and 106," Sheriff Davis said into his radio, "Ready for ya'." He turned his attention back to the men they had at gunpoint, and pulled out his handcuffs. Thankfully, he was prepared and had two sets on him. "Ya' have the right to remain silent. Anything ya' say, can and will be used against ya' in a court of law…," he began.

"We didn't do nothin'," the man who was still standing said.

"We're just doing work for our boss. This is discrimination." His voice grew to a higher pitch as Sheriff Davis slapped the cuffs on him.

"Ya' have the right to an attorney. If ya' can't afford one, one will be appointed fer you," Corey continued, unphased by the man's objections. Meanwhile, the other man was thrashing around on the ground as he cried out in pain.

Two sets of headlights approached the area at high speed coming from opposite ends of the road. The two deputies wasted no time getting there and parking, so that their headlights lit up more of the area. One, a truck as well, had a light bar that they switched on which lit up the entire area.

As the deputies jogged up to assist the sheriff, Brigid let out the breath she hadn't realized she'd been holding. Putting the safety back on and holstering her gun, she looked around the area. She could see where the men had driven up to the storage container before from the beaten-down grass and multiple tire tracks.

Brigid heard the sound of a loud thud coming from the van and turned toward the sheriff and his deputies. "Did you guys hear that?" she asked.

None of them were paying any attention to her, preoccupied with cuffing the suspects and dealing with the one who had been shot and was bleeding. She heard them request an ambulance as she crept closer to the white van. Stepping past the door, she listened closely, wondering if perhaps what she'd heard was only her imagination. That's when she heard it again. Thump.

Moving faster, she went to the back of the van. She began to reach for the handle and then stopped. What about fingerprints? Would hers mess something up if she were to touch it? Putting her hand under her shirt, she used it like a glove to gently pull on the handle, and the door popped open. Once she saw what was inside, she gasped.

"Corey! Come here, now," she cried out as she climbed inside.

Huddled in the corner of the van was a small person with their hands tied behind their back and a hood pulled over their head. Walking hunched over towards the back of the van, Brigid heard Sheriff Davis arrive at the back of the van.

"Oh, my Lord," he said in a hushed tone. He pulled out his flashlight and shined it on the person who was still in the darkness of the van, even with all the lights outside.

The person squealed and tried to retreat farther back, scrambling with a crab-like motion along the floor of the van, despite their arms and legs being bound.

"Shhh," Brigid said softly. "I'm here to help you."

Reaching out, Brigid tugged the hood from the person's face and saw that it was a young girl. She was about Holly's age, maybe a year or two younger. Her dirty blonde hair was tangled. Her eyes were wide with fear until she was able to focus, and then she seemed to calm down. There was a bandana tied around her mouth, keeping her from speaking.

"I'm going to untie you now," Brigid said carefully. In the distance, she heard the approaching ambulance.

"Here's my knife if ya' need it," Sheriff Davis said, as he slid it across the van floor. "I gotta' help my guys load up the bad guys. Help her out, and see if ya' can find out where she's from," he said before walking away.

Brigid untied the bandana from the girl's mouth first.

"Are you okay?" Brigid asked as she pulled it away.

The girl nodded. "I think so."

"What's your name?" Brigid asked gently.

"Kelly Bingham. I'm from Sunset Grove," she squeaked. "I was just walking home and… and," the girl began before she burst into tears.

"Shhh. It's okay, Kelly. You're safe now," Brigid said as she picked up the knife and began cutting at the nylon rope that was looped around the girl's ankles. Once her legs were free, she turned the girl around and cut the rope that was tied to her wrists. "Let's get you out of this van," Brigid said as she helped the girl up.

While they were getting out of the van, one of the deputies returned with Sheriff Davis.

"This is Kelly. She's from Sunset Grove," Brigid told them.

"Hey, Kelly. This is Deputy Schinstock. He's gonna' take ya' down to the sheriff's station. After I take yer' statement there, this lady, Brigid, will call yer' parents," Sheriff Davis said.

The girl gave Brigid one last long look before walking away with the deputy.

"Let's go see what they've been up to in the storage container. Good job on findin' the girl. Seems we were lucky, or she was. Either way, she's gonna' be goin' home after her ordeal, thanks to you," the sheriff said as they walked over to the container.

"I heard her making a thumping sound in the van. I think she must have heard you yell 'Sheriff's Department' and was trying to get our attention," Brigid said. She was still a bit shocked from the whole thing. When she'd opened the van's door, she'd never expected to see a helpless young girl huddled in the corner. The way she'd tried to get away when she heard Brigid drawing closer was seared into Brigid's memory. She wasn't quite sure how she would ever manage to get that out of her mind.

"Still, ya' done good." Sheriff Davis had on black rubber gloves as he reached for the padlock on the door of the storage container. The owner's keys were still hanging from the bottom of it, but the lock had been sprung. The sheriff turned it to the open position and pulled it free before undoing the latch and pulling hard on the door. A loud groan came from the door as it slowly swung open. Inside, all they could see was darkness.

Sheriff Davis pulled his flashlight from his hip and shined it into the inky blackness of the storage container.

"Oh my God," he said. Inside, there were three people sitting up with their hands shading their eyes to block the light from Corey's flashlight. Two were women, roughly in their twenties, while the other one was a young boy who looked to be about eleven. All were dirty and disheveled.

"Olivia? Is that you?" Corey said as he gasped, looking at his friend Mike's wife.

"Corey?" the woman asked as she tried to stand up from the pile of dirty blankets on the floor.

"Take yer' time, Olivia. The rest of ya', too. Ya' can come out now," Sheriff Davis said. "We're with the Sheriff's Department. Y'all are goin' home," he said.

They sobbed and hugged each other before they were strong enough to walk towards the light.

"You were right, Olivia. You told us the sheriff would save us, and he did," said the other woman. Brigid felt herself well up with emotion as the three of them stepped out of the huge metal storage container and out onto the tall grass. Each one looked up at the night sky with tears rolling silently down their cheeks.

CHAPTER TWENTY-ONE

Except for the man who'd been shot, everyone else was transported to the sheriff's station. The wounded man was on his way to the hospital with a deputy to get treatment before heading to jail. The other suspect was locked in the back of a sheriff's patrol car, safely away from everyone else's view.

The deputies headed back out to the field to document the scene, while Brigid and Sheriff Davis went to the sheriff's station to talk to the victims and get official statements from them. The deputies that remained at the crime scene needed to photograph and analyze everything to be sure they built a solid case against the suspects. After seeing the conditions Olivia and the others had been kept in, everyone wanted to make sure the two men would be punished to the fullest extent of the law.

They'd been locked inside the metal storage container with nothing but a bucket to use as a restroom and blankets on the floor. They told Brigid and the others that there were small holes in the ceiling that let in a bit of light, but it had been fairly dark most of the time.

After they'd been transported to the sheriff's station, the three victims who had been locked in the storage container sat in wooden chairs, while Brigid sat behind one of the deputy's desks. Corey told her he was going to take Olivia's statement first, and then those of the three other victims.

Brigid thought it seemed strange to be in the sheriff's station so late in the evening. On other occasions when she'd been there it was a hub of activity with people bustling around and working on one thing or another. Now it was quiet.

"How are you doing, Kelly?" Brigid asked the young girl. Kelly had been nervously chewing on her nails ever since they'd arrived and from the looks of them, probably long before that.

"I'm okay," she said as she pulled the blanket that was draped around her shoulders closer. "Pretty shook up, but I think I'm okay."

"That's good," Brigid said. "How did you end up in the back of that van? What made you bang on the floor?"

"I was walking home from a friend's house. I took a shortcut, because I was running late, and my parents threatened to ground me if I was ever late again. I heard a vehicle coming, but I didn't pay much attention to it. People are always coming and going on that shortcut. No big deal. It wasn't until I heard a door open and saw two men rushing toward me that I knew I was in trouble. I tried to fight them off, but they were too strong and quick. Next thing I knew they had me tied up in the back of the van."

She looked as though she was still in shock, but the fact that she was speaking so clearly was a good sign. "I heard the sheriff call out, so when things got quiet, I started banging my feet on the floor of the van. I was just hoping someone would hear me."

"That's kind of what happened to me, too," the young boy said, speaking up for the first time. He'd been quiet until then.

"What's your name?" Brigid asked as she turned her attention to him.

"Henry," he said softly. "I'm from Great Bend." His lips were a thin line of worry beneath his sunken eyes. The dark hair on his head was matted and dirty, as though it had been a while since he'd had a shower.

"How old are you Henry?" she asked.

"I just turned twelve last month," he said. "I was walking home from school when those guys grabbed me. I had my headphones in, so I never heard anything. I just felt someone grab me, and some kind of a cloth bag was slipped over my head."

"I told you to stay positive, didn't I?" the older woman who was the third person who was held captive said.

The boy nodded and gave her a watery smile. "I did my best," he said softly.

"And you did a great job, Henry. You were brave and strong. Don't ever forget that," she said with a nod.

When Brigid looked at her, she smiled weakly. "I'm June. I also live in Great Bend. I was the first one locked in the storage container. I think I've been in there almost a week, but I'm not really sure. The days started to blur together," she admitted.

"Well, you're safe now, June. Once Sheriff Davis gets a chance to speak with each of you and get your statements, we'll contact your families. You'll be home soon, and you can get some much-needed rest." Brigid could only imagine what these peoples' families must be thinking.

The door to Sheriff Davis' office opened and Olivia walked out. Her eyes were red ringed, as though she'd been crying once again. She also had a blanket wrapped around her shoulders.

"Brigid? Would ya' call Mike, Olivia's husband, and let him know she's safe and with us. Tell him he can come pick her up." He gently touched her back and she turned to look at him. "If I have any more questions, I'll come by."

"Thank you, Corey," she said.

"Who wants to come in next?" he asked.

"Let Henry go next," June said. "I'm sure his parents are worried sick."

"Come on in, Henry. Let's get ya' home," he said as the boy stood up and went into his office. Olivia took the boy's seat next to June.

"I know this might sound crazy," June said to Olivia. "But do you think we might be able to talk from time to time? I think you helped keep me sane." The woman chuckled nervously and Brigid could clearly see the woman was exhausted after her week-long ordeal.

"Of course," Olivia said. "I don't think anyone else besides Henry could understand what we went through in there."

They gave each other a long and meaningful hug before Brigid finally spoke.

"You ready for me to give your husband a call?" she asked.

"Definitely," Olivia sighed. Tears began to form in her eyes again. "I can't wait to see him."

Brigid picked up the phone on the desk and handed it to Olivia to dial. "Let me give him a head's up first. Then I'll let you talk to him. I bet he'll be ecstatic to hear your voice. He was a wreck the day you went missing."

"You know Mike?" Olivia asked, confused.

"I met him the morning you disappeared. My name's Brigid Barnes. You and I were supposed to meet that morning," she said while Olivia dialed.

"Oh, yes! You're getting married soon," she said. "And aren't you also the woman who's helped Corey in the past?"

"One and the same," Brigid said as the phone began to ring.

"Hello?" came a groggy voice on the other end.

"Is this Mike Ford?" Brigid asked.

He cleared his throat. "Yeah, I mean, yes. Who is this?"

"Mike, this is Brigid. We spoke a few days ago, and you asked me to help find your wife," she said as she watched Olivia's face.

"That's right," Mike began.

"Mike, we found Olivia. She's here at the sheriff's department, safe and sound," Brigid said smiling.

"Really? Thank heavens. My prayers have been answered. I'll be there in just a few minutes," he said with enthusiasm.

"Would you like to speak with her?" Brigid asked.

"Y-yes, please," he stammered.

Brigid handed the phone to Olivia, who eagerly took it from her.

"Mike?" she said weakly.

Brigid didn't know what he said, but Olivia's face crumpled as tears again started to slide down her cheeks.

"Yeah, baby. It's me. It's so good to hear your voice." She paused as she listened. "I can't wait for you to get here, but you drive carefully. I know how you are. I love you too, Mike. Always and forever." She made kissy noises into the phone before finally saying, "Yes, just get here, okay. I'm waiting." She sighed as she hung up the phone.

"I'm so glad you're okay," Brigid said, her voice cracking with emotion.

"Me, too," she said, unconsciously touching her belly. Brigid smiled, knowing what she was doing. She wanted to speak up and say she knew, but she held back. It wasn't her secret to share. Olivia hadn't wanted to tell anyone, and Brigid did not want to betray that confidence. Instead, she just let the sight of the woman affectionately rubbing her belly fill her heart with hope.

"Well, I guess I really owe you one," Olivia finally said.

"Don't worry about it, really," Brigid said as she waved her off. "It was my pleasure to help. Besides, your husband asked me to help Corey."

"You still could have said no. You already have a lot on your plate just planning a wedding. You didn't need to spend your time trying to find a woman you didn't even know," Olivia said as she shook her head.

"It seemed like the right thing to do," Brigid said with a shrug.

"I know what I can do to pay you back! Let me make your wedding bouquet for free. It's the least I can do for you helping get me back to my home. I heard the men that took us talking the other day. Once they had four of us, they were going to take us away. If you'd have waited one more day, we might not have been found," Olivia insisted.

The reality of what Olivia had just said hit home with Brigid like a bombshell. Sheriff Davis was always swamped. If she hadn't done the interviews for him, it may have taken him another day to find the kidnappers, and by then, it would have been too late. A cold chill rushed through her body, and she felt like her hair was standing on end. She realized how differently things would have gone for these four people if she hadn't helped the sheriff.

"We can talk about it once you're feeling a little more rested," Brigid finally said. "That will give you a little time in case you want to change your mind."

"I won't. I can promise you that," Olivia said.

The sound of a truck pulling up outside made them all turn. Olivia stood so that she could see over the counter that separated the desks from the entrance. Mike jumped out of his truck and rushed inside the building, his eyes scanning the room for his wife. Once his eyes locked onto hers, he hurried toward her.

"Oh, Olivia. I missed you so much," he said as he pulled her into his arms.

"I missed you too," she squeaked. His mouth found hers and they kissed so long and deep that Brigid felt as though it were only proper to look away.

Finally, after they broke apart, Mike said, "Thank you, Brigid. You really came through for me."

"Corey did most of it, I just did some of the leg work for him," she deferred.

"Still, thank you," he said.

The office door opened, and Henry came walking out with the sheriff.

"Glad to see ya', Mike," Corey said. "Olivia's a sight for sore eyes, ain't she."

Mike turned and looked at her, a smile on his face. "Yes, Corey. I can never thank you and Brigid enough."

"Yer' very welcome. Now ya' take her home and treat her good, ya' hear? I'll be by in a coupla' days," Corey said.

"Look forward to it," Mike said. He turned to Olivia and said. "Let's get you home, babe." With his arm around her as if he was afraid to let go of her, he led her out of the building and helped her up into his truck.

"Now that's what I like to see. A happy endin'," Sheriff Davis said before turning his attention to Kelly and June. "Which one of ya' wants to go next?"

Kelly turned to June, wide-eyed. She looked as if she wanted to say something, but didn't have the courage to.

"Go ahead, honey," June said. "You can head on in."

Kelly didn't think twice before standing and following the sheriff into his office.

"Brigid, go ahead and call Henry's family, if ya' would. Give June's family a ring too, so they can start headin' this way. I'll call this one's family." Brigid gave him a thumbs up before he closed his office door.

"That was awfully nice of you," Brigid said. "You could have gone next."

"I know, but she's just a young and very frightened girl. Plus, she was just snatched tonight. I bet her parents are sick with worry." June sighed as she pushed her dirty brown hair back from her face. "I can't wait to get something good to eat."

"What have you been eating?" Brigid asked.

"Whatever they happened to bring to us. One night it was just a bag of oranges. I always wanted to lose weight, just never thought it would happen this way. I'd kill to have a double cheeseburger right now."

"You ready to call your family?" Brigid asked Henry.

He nodded. "I miss my mom and dad and even my little sister," he admitted, "but a cheeseburger sounds pretty good."

Brigid lifted the phone cradle as she asked Henry to dial his home number. After a few rings, a woman answered.

"Hello?"

"Hello, my name is Brigid, and I'm calling you about Henry," Brigid began.

"Did you find him?" the woman asked as if she were afraid to hope.

"Yes, ma'am. He's right here with me. We're in the Cottonwood Springs Sheriff's Department. If you'd like to come get him, I'm sure he'd love to go home. Would you like to speak with him?" Brigid felt wonderful being able to tell this woman her son was safe.

"Oh, yes. Yes, please. I knew he didn't run away! Phil, Phil, wake up! They've found Henry!" she was saying as Brigid handed the phone to Henry.

"Mom?" he said softly. His eyes began to water and thick tears slipped down his cheeks. "Yeah, I'm okay. Just come get me, okay? I want to come home." He listened for a little longer before finally saying. "I love you, too. Hurry. Bye." He looked up at Brigid. "I can't wait to see them."

"I don't blame you," Brigid said smiling.

"Can I go to the bathroom?" he said, wide eyed.

"Sure, it's just through that door," she said pointing him in the right direction.

"I guess that means it's my turn," June said.

"I guess so," Brigid said. She pushed the phone across the desk. "I think I'll let you do the honors."

"I don't really know who to call first. My mom or my fiancé," she said.

"Call your mom first," Brigid suggested. "I'm sure she's worried out of her mind."

"Yeah, but she doesn't drive well at night," she began.

"Could your fiancé drive her over here?" Brigid asked.

She nodded. "Good idea."

CHAPTER TWENTY-TWO

The big day had finally come. Brigid was excited but nervous. Outside, she could hear people arriving as car doors shut and the sound of friendly conversations grew louder.

Brigid had just stepped into her wedding gown and gotten it pulled up when there was a knock on the bedroom door.

"Come in," she called over her shoulder. Fiona, Holly and Missy all filed into the bedroom. They were already dressed with their hair and makeup done.

"How's it going in here?" Fiona asked, as she hurried over to help Brigid fasten her gown.

"Getting nervous," Brigid admitted as she stood in front of her full-length mirror. She couldn't believe it was her reflection. Her skin was bright and glowing, as if she were emitting a light from within.

"It looks beautiful out there, Brigid," Missy said. "You did a great job planning it all. I don't think you could have made a more beautiful wedding."

"Thank you," Brigid said smiling. "I hope everyone enjoys it as much as you."

"This isn't everyone else's wedding, silly," Fiona teased as she looked at her sister in the mirror. "It doesn't matter if they like it, as long as you do." Fiona was snacking on a slice of apple while they spoke.

"How can you eat right now?" Brigid asked in amazement. "I haven't been able to eat for days."

"Uh, about that," Fiona said as her eyes looked down at the floor and then began darting around nervously.

"What aren't you telling me?" Brigid asked, suddenly panicking.

"Calm down. It's nothing bad," Fiona said quickly. "It's just, I've had something I wanted to tell you, but I've been waiting for the right moment."

"Well spit it out," Brigid said turning to face her sister directly. "You're going to give me an anxiety attack, and that's the last thing I need right now."

"You know how you've noticed I've been snacking a lot more, recently?" she began. Brigid, as well as Holly and Missy were hanging on her every word.

"Yes?" Brigid said, drawing the word out.

"That's because I'm pregnant," she said, her voice breaking at the end. She began fanning herself, holding back tears.

"Are you serious?" Brigid asked, shocked.

"Yeah, I didn't want to announce it at your wedding, but I just can't hold it in any longer." She smiled and then laughed. "You're going to be an aunt."

"That's wonderful!" Brigid said as she pulled her sister into her arms. "Congratulations!"

Holly and Missy were also excitedly hugging her, happy to share in the great news on such an important day.

A knock on the door made them turn as Brigid said, "Come in."

"Everyone's here," said Sheriff Davis. "Y'all 'bout ready?"

"We're ready," Missy said nodding. "Tell Jordan he can start."

Corey nodded as he ducked back out of the room.

"Here we go," Fiona said.

The four of them made their way outside, going the way they'd practiced the previous day at the rehearsal. The temporary lattice wall covered in vines and flowers hid them from the guests until the music began to play. Soon, one by one, they started walking down the aisle.

"Make sure you breathe," Fiona said as Missy began walking down the aisle. It was just Brigid and Fiona left, and she could tell Brigid was getting super nervous. She picked up the bouquet of white and red roses and handed them to Brigid. "Remember, everyone out there is either friends or family. Don't think too much about it. You're going to be just fine."

"Thank you, Fiona," Brigid said. "For everything. For talking me into coming back here. If I hadn't, I would have never met Linc or Holly…" she let her sentence trail off, as she began to feel the prickling of tears in her eyes.

"Don't mention it," Fiona shrugged. "Oh, it's my turn." She took her place at the starting point of the aisle and with one last smile toward Brigid, she began her march.

"Here we go," Brigid said aloud to herself. "It's no big deal. Just don't trip, and don't forget to breathe."

She adjusted her dress one last time and swiped a finger under each eye to make sure her eyeliner hadn't started to run before finally plastering a smile on her face. At first, it was fake. Yet, as she stepped up to the aisle and the music changed, it became very, very real.

Each guest stood as she started down the grassy aisle deeply littered with red rose petals. The guests were all smiling and taking pictures as she slowly walked down the aisle. She noticed the deputies, and that June and Olivia were sitting next to each other, with Mike next to her. She also spotted Eve Sterling with her husband, as well as many other friends and acquaintances from around the small town. She felt so very blessed to have so many people wanting to share her big day with her. It was like a dream come true.

When she looked farther down the aisle, she saw Linc. His brother had flown in to be his best man and a couple of his friends also stood up with him. But Brigid only had eyes for Linc. Standing there, with a broad grin on his face, Brigid couldn't help but think she was the luckiest woman alive. He looked so handsome in his suit with a red rose pinned to his lapel. She had to make a serious effort to keep from grinning like a fool as she headed toward the altar.

The only thing that kept running through Brigid's mind was, *Don't trip, don't trip, don't trip.* It was as if it were on one continuous loop. *Don't trip, don't trip, don't trip. Please, please, please. Don't trip, don't trip, don't trip.*

She didn't relax until she was standing across from Linc.

"Hey," he said with his lopsided smile.

"Hey, yourself," she said, laughing slightly.

"Fancy meeting you here," Linc joked just before Jordan began the ceremony.

"Friends and family, Linc and Brigid invited all of you here today to witness their commitment to each other. They've asked that we keep the ceremony short and sweet, so that everyone can spend more time enjoying themselves and the festivities.

"I would just like to say how reassuring it is to see two people so very much in love. While their paths may have had some detours in getting here, I think I can speak for everyone when I say that it's plain these two were meant for each other. Sometimes we need to learn certain lessons before we can be with our true other half. This may come in the form of other marriages or what have you.

"But love cannot be stopped. It will move mountains to bring two people who are meant to be together. Love is patient, and knows nothing of time. Love is faithful, so that no matter what happens, you know it will always be there. And finally, love is devotion. Being there for one another against all odds, no matter what life throws at you.

"So today, we witness Brigid Barnes and Linc Olsen committing to spend the rest of their lives together. Are you two ready to say your vows?" he asked as he looked at them. When they both nodded, he said, "Linc, you may go first."

Linc took the ring and cleared his throat before beginning to slide it on Brigid's finger.

"Brigid, I never thought I could love another person the way I love you. It's all consuming, I can't take a breath without feeling my heart swell at the thought of you. Just knowing you want to be with me makes me the happiest man on earth. I couldn't ask for more. I'll spend the rest of my days waking up and thanking God for the opportunity to be your husband.

"It had to be fate that brought me here. That's the only thing that seems to make sense. Of all the places I could have gone, I landed right here, next door to you. If that's not meant to be, I don't know what is." He smiled as he pushed the ring all the way onto her finger.

"Brigid?" Jordan asked as he handed her the ring.

"Linc, you've opened my eyes to what love can really be. Before I met you, I didn't understand it, not really. And I used to scoff at those romantic films, because I thought they were all unrealistic. But you showed me they aren't. That good men do exist and now, I get to marry one. You've accepted me for who I am. No questions, no expectations. You saw who I was and decided to love me anyway. I know there's nothing I can't get through with you by my side. You are quite literally my other half. We complement each other so well, I don't know how I made it through my life without you. I'm just glad that now, I don't have to do that anymore. As long as we're together, I'm happy."

"Beautiful words," Jordan said. "Now, do you, Linc Olsen take Brigid Barnes to be your wedded wife? To have and to hold, in sickness and in health, from this day forward, as long as you both shall live?"

"I do," Linc said, beaming.

"And you, Brigid Barnes. Do you take Linc Olsen to be your wedded husband? To have and to hold, in sickness and in health, from this day forward, as long as you both shall live?"

"I do," Brigid grinned.

"Then I now pronounce you husband and wife. You may kiss the bride!"

Linc reached for Brigid and kissed her just like the first time. She swore her foot lifted from the ground as their mouths met, symbolically joining them for the rest of their lives.

EPILOGUE

"Are you about ready?" Brigid called down the hall. Holly's door was still closed, and she could hear her banging around inside her bedroom.

"Don't worry, we have plenty of time," Linc said soothingly as he caressed Brigid's back.

"I know, I just like to leave early. You know how bad the traffic in Denver can be," she said.

"It will all work out," Linc said. "You'll see. Not everyone has to be places super early," he teased. He picked up their suitcases and headed for the front door. "I'm going to go ahead and load these up while we wait." When he opened the door he said, "Fiona's here," before stepping outside. Fiona walked through the door and shut it behind her.

"How does it feel to be a married woman again?" she asked as she hugged her sister.

"Stressful. I swear, I don't think we're ever going to get to the airport," Brigid said, as she collected the dog leash and the bag where she'd packed all of Jett's toys. "I packed his toys up, so he'd have something familiar. I'll have Linc carry out the dog food bag when he comes back in. Have Brandon unload it, it's heavy. It should be enough to get him through our vacation honeymoon, but if it isn't, just let me know what I owe you when I get back."

"Not even worried about it," Fiona said. "I'm just excited to be able to spend some time alone with him. After all, he did save my life," she said referring to when someone had recently tried to kill her.

"That he did. Enjoy him," Brigid said as Holly finally emerged from her room.

"Hey Fiona," Holly said. She walked over to the big dog and scratched his head. "I'm going to miss you when I'm gone, Jett," she said talking to him in baby talk.

"What about me?" Fiona asked, pretending her feelings were hurt. She stuck out her lower lip as if she were pouting.

"You too, of course," she said smiling and giving Fiona a hug. "Try to take it easy while we're gone. No heavy lifting or crazy rearranging while I'm away. If you want something changed in the bookstore, I can do it when I get back."

"I will, and you have fun, kiddo. I want to see pictures when you come back. Send me messages and stuff, too. I want to know what you're up to," Fiona said hugging her back and kissing her forehead.

"No problem," Holly said. "I gotta' go load up my bags," she said as she carried her backpack and suitcase outside.

"How are all the people doing that were kidnapped?" Fiona asked.

"Good," Brigid said. "I'm sure you've heard by now that Olivia told Mike she was pregnant."

"Who wouldn't know? The fact that he tells everyone he comes across has spread the news like wildfire," Fiona chuckled.

"I know," Brigid laughed. "But I'm happy for them. The other woman, June, she's doing well. I heard she's writing a book about her whole ordeal."

"Wow, maybe if she gets it published, she can come talk at the bookstore," Fiona suggested.

"That's not a bad idea," Brigid commented. "I heard both Henry and Kelly are doing okay, too. Still a little shaken up, but healthy and moving on with their lives."

"Good, I'm so glad. Well, I'll get out of your hair. Come on, Jett. Let's go," Fiona said as she hooked his leash on his collar. Jett happily followed her to the door while Brigid trailed behind.

Linc came in and grabbed the bag of food before heading back outside and putting it in the back of Fiona's car. They all waved to Jett and Fiona as they pulled away.

"Everyone ready?" Linc asked.

"Let me check the house one more time and then we can go," Brigid said.

Linc and Holly finished loading up in the truck as they waited for Brigid.

"Are you nervous?" Linc asked.

"Kind of," Holly admitted. "I've never flown before."

"It's not that bad," he said. "Some people get nervous during the takeoff and the landing, but for me, that's the best part."

"Yeah, but you're weird," Holly said laughing.

"You have a point," he said. "But your flight won't last too long. You'll be there in no time."

"I hope so," she said.

Brigid rushed out the front door, checking it to make sure it was locked, before jogging to the truck.

"Okay, I'm ready," she said.

*****

"I'm going to miss you guys," Holly said as they stood outside the boarding gate for her flight.

"We'll miss you, too," Brigid said. "Try to have lots of fun, though."

"Yeah, and make sure you give them a chance. You just never know, you may end up enjoying yourself," Linc said giving her a wink.

Holly laughed. "You're right Linc, you just never know," she said. "And you guys have fun, too. She looked at Linc and mock whispered, "Try to keep Brigid out of trouble. You know how she is about finding trouble wherever she goes."

Linc smiled. "I'll do my best, but I agree, you know how she is," he said with a shrug.

"That I do," she said. "I love you guys. See you soon." Holly turned and walked toward the gate, pausing only once to look back and wave.

"Do you think she'll be okay?" Brigid asked with a sound of concern in her voice as she leaned into Linc.

"Definitely," he said. "Don't worry about her. She's got a good head on her shoulders, and you've had an amazing positive influence on her. She'll be totally fine."

"I'm just worried she won't like it and want to come home. There's no guarantee our cell phones will work. What if she tries to get in touch with us, and she can't?" Brigid said as she began to worry.

"She can call Fiona. Brigid, calm down. Do you want to go on this trip or not?"

"Of course," she said, looking surprised. Realizing she had been overreacting, she took a deep breath and smiled. "I'm sorry."

"You're fine," Linc said. "Just let it all go, because now the honeymoon begins."

RECIPES

SEARED SCALLOPS & PASTA IN ALFREDO SAUCE

Ingredients:
12 sea scallops (fresh or frozen; if frozen thaw first)
1 tsp. unsalted butter
1 tsp olive oil
½ cup cream
½ cup shredded Parmesan cheese
½ cup unsalted butter
Lemon pepper to taste (I like Lawry's, but any will do.)
½ box fettucine pasta

Directions:
Cook pasta in boiling water per instructions on the box.

In a small saucepan combine cream, Parmesan cheese, and butter to make Alfredo sauce and cook over medium heat until just melted, then turn burner to low until pasta and scallops are finished.

Pat the scallops dry and season with lemon pepper. Add butter and olive oil to a large frying pan over medium high heat. Add the scallops one at a time, flat side down (you can use your fingers to do this), and sear until just turning golden brown (about 2 minutes). Using tongs, flip each scallop individually and sear the other flat side until golden brown (about another 2 minutes). Caution: Don't overcook the scallops or they will become tough.

Slide the cooked scallops out of the frying pan and add directly to the saucepan containing the Alfredo sauce. Stir and combine so scallops are well covered with sauce. Drain the cooked pasta and plate it. Pour half the scallop/Alfredo mixture directly over each of the 2 plated pastas, allocating 6 scallops per serving. Serve & enjoy!

NOTE: This recipe serves two. If a larger serving is required, allocate 6 scallops per person and increase pasta and Alfredo sauce proportionally. (You can make the Alfredo sauce in any amount you want, just combine the 3 ingredients in equal amounts and heat as directed).

QUICK PEANUT BUTTER COOKIES

Ingredients:

1 cup crunchy peanut butter
½ cup sugar
1 egg

Directions:

Preheat oven to 350 degrees. Mix ingredients together. Place teaspoonfuls of dough on unbaked cookie sheet (I prefer to line the cookie sheet with parchment paper, but if you don't have any, no problem). Bake 12-15 minute, being careful not to overcook. Enjoy!

NOTE: No, I didn't forget to include flour because none is required in this recipe!

WARM STEAK SALAD WITH SHERRIED CHERRIES

Ingredients:

1 boneless steak such as rib-eye, flat iron, strip, or hanger
¾ cup fresh or frozen pitted cherries

4 tbsp. sherry vinegar (If you don't have it, make your own by mixing 1:1 sherry and white vinegar.)
3 tbsp. olive oil, divided
3 cups loosely packed arugula (You can buy this in a plastic container in the ready to eat salad section of your supermarket.)
3 tbsp. sliced almonds
1/3 of a red onion, sliced thin, outer rings only, cut in bite-sized pieces, about 1 1/2 – 2"in length)

Directions:

Generously season both sides of steak with salt and pepper or your favorite BBQ rub and allow to rest for 15 minutes before cooking.

Meanwhile in a small saucepan over low heat, combine the cherries, sherry vinegar, and pinch of salt. Warm for a few minutes, and then set aside to soak while you cook the steak.

Heat a large cast iron skillet over medium-high heat until it is nearly smoking, then swirl in 1 tbsp. olive oil. Place steak in skillet and brown on one side for about 4 minutes.

Flip & cook on the second side to your preferred doneness, 3-4 minutes for medium rare. Transfer steak to cutting board and let rest 3-4 minutes for medium rare. Add remaining olive oil to sherried cherries mixture.

Toss arugula and onions in large salad bowl while adding sherried cherries mixture until well coated. Remove salad mixture from salad bowl and place a single serving on each diner plate. Sprinkle with sliced almonds. Slice steak against the grain into bite-size slices and scatter on top of salad. Enjoy!

EASY BAKED FRIES

Ingredients:

1 large baking potato, unpeeled

2 tbsp. olive oil
½ tsp. paprika
½ tsp. garlic powder
2 -3 drops of Tabasco
½ tsp. onion powder

Directions:
Preheat oven to 450 degrees. Cut potato into thin wedges. Mix olive oil, paprika, garlic powder, Tabasco, and onion powder together. Coat potato with oil/spice mixture and place on baking sheet. Bake for 45 minutes in oven. Enjoy!

BUTTERSCOTCH/BLONDIE BARS

Ingredients:
1/4 cup butter
1 cup brown sugar
1 egg
1 tsp. vanilla
1/2 cup all-purpose flour
1 tsp. baking powder
1/2 tsp. salt
3/4 cup sweetened coconut (comes in a plastic package)

Directions:
Preheat oven to 350 degrees. Lightly grease a 9" x 9" pan.

Melt butter in a saucepan over medium-low heat. Stir the brown sugar into the melted butter and set aside to cool slightly. When the butter mixture has cooled slightly, beat in the egg and vanilla.

Sift the flour, then resift with the baking powder and salt. Mix flour mixture into the sugar mixture. Add the coconut.

Pour batter into prepared dish and bake for 20-25 minutes. When cool, cut into bars. Enjoy!

Paperbacks & Ebooks for FREE

Go to www.dianneharman.com/freepaperback.html and get your FREE copies of Dianne's books and favorite recipes immediately by signing up for her newsletter.

Once you've signed up for her newsletter you're eligible to win three paperbacks. One lucky winner is picked every week. Hurry before the offer ends!

ABOUT THE AUTHOR

Dianne lives in Huntington Beach, California, with her husband, Tom, a former California State Senator, and her boxer dog, Kelly. Her passions are cooking, reading, and dogs, so whenever she has a little free time, you can either find her in the kitchen, playing with Kelly in the back yard, or curled up with the latest book she's reading.

Her award winning books include:

Cedar Bay Cozy Mystery Series

Cedar Bay Cozy Mystery Series - Boxed Set

Liz Lucas Cozy Mystery Series

Liz Lucas Cozy Mystery Series - Boxed Set

High Desert Cozy Mystery Series

High Desert Cozy Mystery Series - Boxed Set

Northwest Cozy Mystery Series

Northwest Cozy Mystery Series - Boxed Set

Midwest Cozy Mystery Series

Midwest Cozy Mystery Series - Boxed Set

Jack Trout Cozy Mystery Series

Cottonwood Springs Cozy Mysteries

Coyote Series

Midlife Journey Series

Red Zero Series

Black Dot Series

Newsletter

If you would like to be notified of her latest releases please go to www.dianneharman.com and sign up for her newsletter.

Website: www.dianneharman.com,
Blog: www.dianneharman.com/blog
Email: dianne@dianneharman.com

PUBLISHING 2/27/19

SMALL TOWN MURDER

BOOK SEVEN OF

THE MIDWEST COZY MYSTERY SERIES

http://getBook.at/STM

Kat only wanted to be part of the convention on how to write successful books, not solve a murder that took place there – the murder of a beloved "tell-all" author. Was that the motive?

Greed, revenge, and hatred are also reasons to murder, at least to people who live on the slippery edge of sanity. Parsons who gamble, women who blackmail, and a number of people with outsized egos make for most interesting characters.

And yet, even with the worst of human nature, miracles can happen.

If you like to feel good at the end of a book, with maybe a tear or two and a smile, don't miss this inspirational story with plenty of dogs, food, and recipes.

Open your smartphone, point and shoot at the QR code below. You will be taken to Amazon where you can pre-order 'Small Town Murder'.

(Download the QR code app onto your smartphone from the iTunes or Google Play store in order to read the QR code below.)

Made in the USA
Monee, IL
23 December 2021